Thin Windows

A Narrative Collection
R.E. Lockett

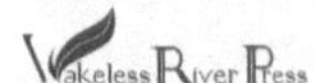

Wakeless River Press

Thin Windows
R. E. Lockett

Published by Wakeless River Press LLC, USA
Printed in the United States of America

Library of Congress Control Number: 2024920281
ISBN:
978-1-955564-07-6 - Paperback
978-1-955564-08-3 - Ebook

1st edition – 2025

For Landon and Corinne, who light up my life and whose voices are my favorite sounds.

Unfiltered light,
Unburdened views,
And all the sounds
Just hurtle through
Thin windows.

A world of tales,
Most yet untold,
Of life and love
And blood and gold.
Thin windows.

From mind and voice
These truths are birthed.
We judge their use
And weigh their worth
In windows.

Dividing minds,
But hiding naught.
Clear barriers.
Inside we've got
Thin windows.

Warping in heat,
Or frosted white.
In orange morn,
Or dark of night.
Thin windows.

The fragile glass
Vibrates the tones
That help us feel
Far less alone.
Thin windows.

Contents

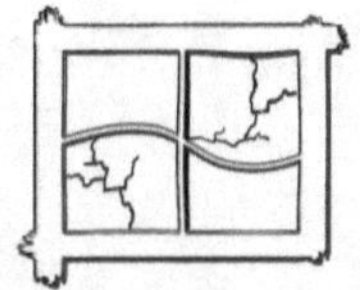

THE RED WOOD

"Will you dew the grass with me?"
She pulls her waders to her knees,
Watching his face with pangs of grief.
He waves her off to her relief.
The sun sits waiting for the morn.

Sprinkling while she skips along,
She sings aloud a joyous song.
The sun joins in with dancing rays,
Illuminating where she plays
And hides away from hunters' horns.

Hunters, well aware of her,
Have placed a price upon her fur.
The woodsman feels the trouble nigh
And so lets loose the mournful sigh
Of one who's seen the throes of war.

Suns make mist the morning dew-

A fog hung just for dancing through.
It's cut through by a hunter's eyes.
He aims his arrow at his prize
To cease her dancing evermore.

Though he thinks the two alone,
A horn rings out and rattles bones.
The frantic fog-dancer retreats
On hooves where once were hands and feet
And disappears from hunter's sight.

Legends told time and again
Of shapeshifters who look like men
Have drawn these hunters to the glade.
Now confirmation has been made
Much to the predator's delight.

Arrows pierce the veil of mist
From all directions that exist.
Echoing horns reverberate
Throughout the woods - the sound of fate.
Echoing, too, the sound of war.

War, it has a certain pull.
The woodsman stands in armor full.
The fawn springs forth. He lets her pass.
Some sands escape the hourglass
To lie there on the forest floor.

Roaring, raising up his axe,
He raises, too, the hair on backs.
Some give in to the fear and run.
For most, the hunt has just begun.
The girl returns to human form.

Anger burns her cheeks aglow.
She dons her ancient antler bow
And armor made to rearrange
Should she see need, again, to change
While dancing through the arrow storm.

Dancing like a dragonfly
Through drops of rain that fill the sky,
She capers through the killing swarm.
The sun dips low, the air grows warm.
The woodsman drinks the shadows in.

Shadows seem to fill his eyes.
He fills his lungs and grows in size.
His axe turns black and grows as well.
He strikes it twice to ring the knell
Then wipes some shadow from his chin.

Empty quivers, shaking hands.
The bravest plan to make a stand.

The fawn-girl fires arrows back.
The woodsman winds up his attack.
The wisest hunters turn and flee.

Arrows suddenly appear
Where fingertip and string draw near.
With rabbit speed, her volley flies
To meet with hearts and throats and eyes
And spill their blood and soak the trees.

Cleaving all within his reach,
He prays beneath his breath for each
Yet still cuts through the men like weeds.
The woodsman fells, the shadow feeds.
A captive and his famished chains.

In the distance terror rings.
His master severing loose strings.
Though most will die with mouths agape,
She will permit one to escape
And call more hunters to be slain.

As it was, as it shall be.
For once a hunter, too, was he.
Admired for his speed and strength,
He'd stalked her through these woods at length
And wisely tracked her by the dew.

Dew is fleeting, shadows stay.
The sun cannot burn them away
For they belonged to Shadowloch,
Protector of the changeling flock,
Once captive of the forest, too.

Shadowloch, the watchful eye,
Could never let a changeling die.
Thus, when the woodsman found his prey,
A battle raged for seven days
With shadows watching from the trees.

Broken was the fawn's defense.
Her power drained, her eyes immense.
The axe had been raised overhead.
A curse on changelings had been said
So loudly it drowned out her pleas.

Down came axe head sharp and swift.
He hadn't seen the shadows shift.
His eyes locked tightly on the girl's,
He'd missed the soot-black coils and curls
Of shadow tendrils creeping in.

Sight itself was sucked away
Between the hunter and his prey.
The axe had buried in the ground
And laughter had replaced the sound

Of pleading from the alter-skin.

Swallowing the urge to scream
While drowning in the tidal stream
Of shadows, darkness, and despair,
The woodsman grew keenly aware
That he was being driven mad.

Will is all a woodsman needs.
The trees don't fall, the wood concedes.
With shadows clawing fore and aft,
He'd gripped the axe's wooden shaft
And spun with all the might he had.

Shadowloch was torn in two.
A valley left for stepping through.
Alas, though, magic never dies
It merely strikes a compromise
With whosoever tips the scale.

Siphoned of his energy,
The woodsman fell to bended knee.
Before him bloomed a path of dew.
The sower come to reap, he knew.
There always was a chance he'd fail.

Wondrous woodsman, woe is he.

Inherited true misery.
The changeling hollowed out his chest
And poured in Shadowloch to rest
And feed upon the woodsman's soul.

Some souls simply won't be still.
The woodsman fought with all his will,
But each by then was far too weak.
Forever they are forced to seek
The other half to make them whole.

Changeling magic takes a toll.
By chaining shadows to his soul
His body lives for her to guide
And all the while he dies inside.
A thin container of a man.

Out he calls his warning yell
And rings his weapon like a bell
When each new hunting pack arrives
To turn them back and save their lives
And starve the shadows if he can.

Shadows weaken, chains can break.
All through the night he lies awake
Wishing the shadows hadn't fed
And lingered in the light instead
That he may once again be free.

Free to kill her. Free to lie
In sun, away from dew, and die.
Let axe and armor rust away.
Escape, if only through decay.
A more than fitting apogee.

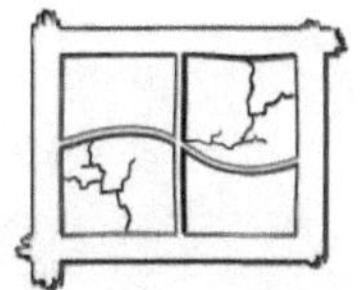

WATERWORKS

R.E. LOCKETT

Crated circles of reconstructed constant
Still being built to be adorned.
Tainted memories of tasteful trips torn down
Will mark my time-true treks no more.
Pavilions and promises placed neatly over
Dancing dams and crying cliffs,
Asking me where I put those paths
To tackle boxes, spiral staircases.

Cannonball blues in the daytime,
Dark in the night breeze; churning water
Fish on the floor, sheep in the sky.
Wishes wearing down on dreamers' daughters.
Fragments of the Old Mill House
Open wide my mouth with curiosity.
How did "Star" Alpalca Braids play into our industrial age?
How did it come to be?

1815, 1909, tell Frederick Graft the water's fine.
Walk the gardens, walk through time.

Bring back the White Perch, Small Mouth Bass, Catfish, Carp,
American Shad. All just in my mind.
Crisscrossed bridges bathe as boathouse row remains
Enslaved and tired.
A single, sad boat on this waste river floats
As I sit on this rock, inspired.

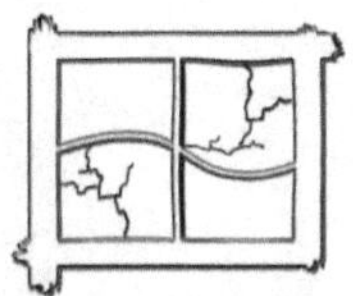

NEW LONDON

New London
Needs a new detective
This man
Just looks at things
Grunts
Takes notes

His partner
Far less introspective
Talks loud
Wears pinky rings
Swears
Emotes

New cases
In this jurisdiction
Go cold
Like winter nights
Freeze
In time

Witnesses
Offer not but fiction
White lies
Truth satellites
Frowns
More crime

New London
Needs a vigilante

New London
Needs an intervention
Docktown
It suffocates
Chokes
Takes life

The people
Live with apprehension
Draw shades
Dilapidate
Sink
In strife

Inspectors
From adjacent cities
Call this
New Murdertown
Laugh

Shake heads

They gesture
Say "Life isn't pretty."
Laugh more
Don't stick around
Flee
Instead

New London
Needs a vigilante

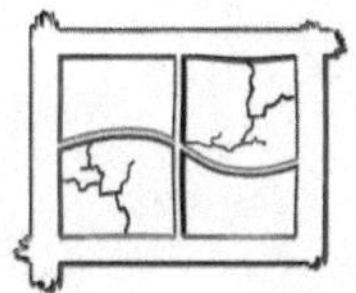

THE CLEANER

I can move it.
I can push and pull
From there to here
The whole of the space trash Dyson sphere.
I can shadow the globe, burn the seas with a nudge.
Even death would budge.
Some days I think I should.
I should burn away the seas.
No one sees.
No one but me.
It is all just a game to them,
Fun, wild, and free.
They can blow up their ships,
Let the pieces float free,
Then blast off in any direction they please.
There will be no obstructions, no trash, no debris.
It is harder work than work should be.
No one sees but me.
No one sees.
No one sees me.

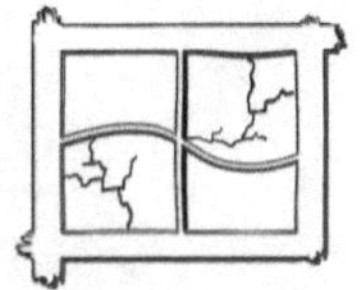

BITTER ALMONDS

Wars don't end anymore these days.
They trick the trap of time
While we all slowly fade away.
Hold your head up high, don't cry, be brave.
If this is staying dry
I'll take my chances with the rain.

One glass of water ought to do.
It's easy going down
When there ain't nothing left to lose.
Clearheaded, just a bit confused.
The path that I have found
Is not the path I meant to choose.

These bitter almonds,
Hard to notice lest you know.
These bitter almonds,
I forgot the antidote.

I feel my brain can hardly breathe.

My eyes are rolling back.
My soul is slowly losing speed.
If I'm not scared, then why do I flee?
There's time left to react.
Maybe this life is what I need.

Can't stop the noises in my head.
I try to meditate
But I keep drawing blanks instead.
Find quiet when I'm fin'ly dead.
'Till then procrastinate,
Try to remember what I read.

These bitter almonds,
Hard to notice lest you know.
These bitter almonds,
I forgot the antidote.

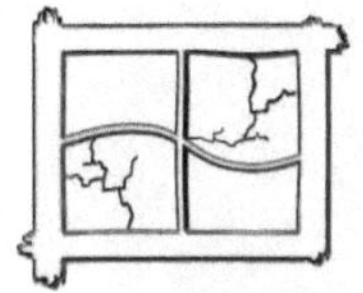

CAMPERDOWN

If not for fear, would they have cowered
Beneath the Camperdown at midnight
With green grass stains around their ankles
And trembling arms around each other
Or would they have been there regardless
Drawn out into the cold and darkness

They'd always been afraid of darkness
Afraid that maybe something cowered
And waited for them to be guard-less
So it could murder them at midnight
When they could not protect each other
Like snakes in grass awaiting ankles.

Bloodsucking bugs bit at their ankles
And stole away into the darkness
One offered her socks to the other
Ready to die right where they cowered
And never see another midnight
She knew that she would die regardless

For father would find them regardless

Beneath the tree, scratching their ankles
And lock them up again till midnight
Inside a room with not but darkness
And one corner in which they cowered
Afraid to let go of each other

Afraid that one would lose the other
One day they'll separate regardless
A tiny thought that's always cowered
Below their chins, above their ankles
Inside their stomachs, deep in darkness
Beside a star of hope, their midnight

And thus, they run away each midnight
And hold on tightly to each other
Hiding, each night, out in the darkness
Knowing that he'll find them regardless
And drag them both back by their ankles
And beat them, for he is a coward

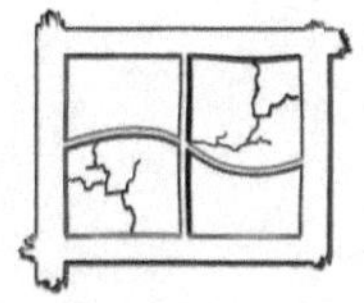

EVERMOURN

I can honestly say
I remember the day
Like Atlantis remembers the moon.
With this thought I have played long since peace went away
On that day that determined my doom.
Been so long since I prayed, I can feel God's dismay,
But religion can't satiate gloom.
Forever mourn for Evermourn.
Her children died too soon.

We all chose to reside
On the Shore of Lost Tides
To pay homage to those who went down
When Atlantis sank into the sea for its sins,
But the sea never could keep the drowned.
When the fishermen set and then checked empty nets
For a month panic spread through the town.
Forever mourn for Evermourn
And all the pain she found.

I was torn from a dream
By the terrible scream
Of a nightwatchman shaking with fear.
Something rattled his brain so he couldn't explain
But hoof prints in the sand made it clear.
Soon the well-rotted corpse of the sea swallowed horse
That had frightened the man reappeared.
Forever mourn for Evermourn
For her the skies were blear.

From the shore children shied.
Lack of trust in the tide
And a fear of what may lie below
Took away any need for rules they wouldn't heed.
There are some things that children just know.
Those accustomed to steel traded scabbard for reel
As we felt further misgivings grow.
Forever mourn for Evermourn,
Caught in the undertow.

We built barricades in
To the sand to begin
To feel safer though none felt secure.
So we fashioned a wall (one mast deep, seven tall)
And set archers atop to be sure.
Those of us most alarmed felt that all should be armed,
But the council felt that premature.
Forever mourn for Evermourn.
Her heart was far too pure.

With no fish caught for feasts
We sent traders back east
With what treasures we found in the sand.
They returned with both bows and the corn for the rows
We had dug down to soil by hand.
With some beach-gathered shells we made arrows as well.
Food and safety were high in demand.
Forever mourn for Evermourn.
Together we did band.

Quiet nights didn't keep,
Like the solace of sleep,
There was never a chance it would stay.
Whether something appeared, or not, moonlight and fear,
Would force screams to chill bones anyway.
Traders sent for more bows. Archers lined up in rows,
Taking rest only during the day.
Forever mourn for Evermourn.
How heavy hearts can weigh.

I had just reached the gates
When the old barricade
Turned to splinters like shattering glass.
Through the smoldering hole flowed the men without souls
So, we beat a retreat to the pass.
It was there that we planned Evermourn's final stand
But the enemies followed too fast.
Forever mourn for Evermourn.
That day our numbers halved.

Through the pass I did slip
Just before the traps tripped
Cutting off our enemy's path.
Had I chosen to stay and make sure we were safe
Less would lie dead with arrow-pierced backs.
Arrows withered and blue, some with heads rusted through,
Others rotting from fletching to shaft.
Forever mourn for Evermourn.
She suffered fore and aft.

Age became a hard line.
We decided that time
Was the best way to choose who would fight.
Any person who'd lived more than twelve years would give
Hope to youth by expressing their might.
Desperation has teeth. The rope's end we had reached.
Still, we held the line well through the night.
Forever mourn for Evermourn,
Her penance, and her plight.

When I finally lay
Down my sword, it was day
And the dead had forgotten to rise.
All round me was pain, death, and sand full of stains.
We had held them off to my surprise.
I tried standing but found dying holds a man down.
So, I settled for whispered goodbyes.
Forever mourn for Evermourn,
But leave her where she lies.

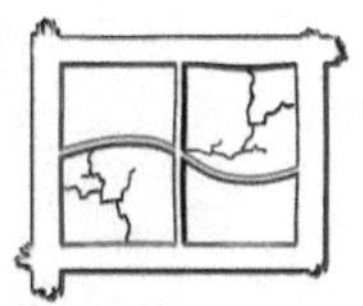

AGE

After a certain age
They come to you.
They ask about your family,
Funny, they are your friends.
They question, subtly, your finances,
Any unfinished business.
After a certain age
They come for you.
They talk to you and lead you away.
They take you to a throne of sorts.
It is adorned
As you are adorned:
So lavishly it seems wasteful.
There are others there
On other thrones
All gaudily bejeweled.
The others were led here by their friends.
They are the same as you.
They sit on their thrones
And eat their favorite meals

As you signal for seconds of yours.
After a certain age they seat you
On your throne
And pull the switch.
After a certain age
You're just taking up space.
After a certain age
You must go away.
When we were very young
We would joke about it.
I remember
We would call it
'Geriatric Shock'.
After a certain age
It isn't funny anymore.
Now,
As I near that age,
I realize that I haven't much time left for laughing.
It is supposed to be an honor to be led away.
Here, trapped in my aging state,
I would rather run away.
After a certain age,
It comes to you.

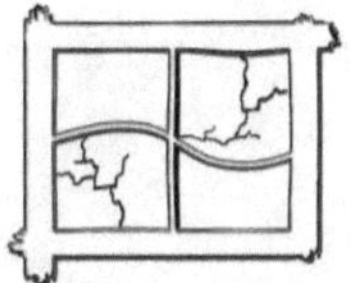

FEATHERWEIGHT

Against my better judgment,
I leaned into the wind.
I let my instincts guide me
And flew out of my skin.
Without my bones and body,
Became only a soul.
Without the weight of sadness,
Completely lost control.
The winds spiraled me higher
And gravity let go.
I flew too close to Heaven.
God said "Look out below!"
I tried to spot my body
But couldn't see the ground.
It's just as well, I gather.
These winds won't let me down.

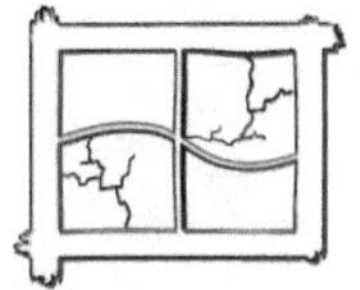

THE LOST AND THE LIGHT

48

I.

An amber night,
Lit both by moon
And by the glow of torches,
Had called us out like hunters hounds
With screaming to enforce it.
The night had swallowed many men
In murky river waters.
Depositing them on the banks
For mothers, wives, and daughters.

Sir Forager
Of Parker Square,
By way of Bridder's Quarry,
Had been found floating near the docks.
A reoccurring story.
A coroner was on the scene
Along with two inspectors,

And, though the wife was in distress,
They all chose to neglect her.

Arriving by
A carriage pulled
By horses with ambition,
We turned the corner just in time
To see the apparition.
Above the Widow Forager,
More smoke than solid being:
A face twisted in agony
That sent bystanders fleeing.

The horses, spooked,
Could not be calmed.
The apparition faded.
And as it did, the panic ceased.
A scene most complicated.
For all who had borne witness then
Seemed suddenly affected
By short-term loss of memory.
A case most unexpected.

As criminal
Consultant for
The New London Observer
I'd spent the whole of my career
Investigating murders.
My good friend and competitor,
Miss Lucille Antoine Courter,

Had spent the same duration with
The New London Reporter.

More oft than not
We'd been assigned,
By editors uncaring,
Identical intention briefs,
Which lent itself to sharing.
Most interviews were joint affairs
With notes compared just after.
And New London's detectives were
A constant source of laughter.

This matter, far
More serious,
Had left us both quite shaken.
The sole owners of memories
We knew were not mistaken.
The stories we'd been sent to write
We knew would now be fiction.
While promising to find the truth
We blamed a false affliction.

The 'heart attack'
Would take two more
And drop them in the river.
The truth could not be further from
The stories we delivered.
And all the while we worked to find
The victims' common tether.

Aside from lying in the morgue
They'd not been seen together.

L.A. and I
Patrolled the docks
Both wanting and not wanting
Some further confirmation of
This thing that we were hunting.
The scenes of all three victims had
Been equally upsetting:
The widows and the panic and
The people all forgetting.

On microfiche,
Down in the depths
Of archives dark and dreary,
We searched New London's history
While working on a theory.
A pattern rose like fingerprints
On microfilm mishandled.
Twelve deaths in half as many years,
All men entrenched in scandal.

No lost recall
Or floating heads
Were mentioned in the sources,
Though one descriptive article
Made note of frightened horses.
The article was from The Post,
A rag best known for slander.

The byline pointed to a man
Named Fernwood, Alexander.

II.

The Fernwood home
Stands all alone
Atop a hill in Stonehurst.
Its garden shriveled, dead and dry,
Just like its murdered owners.
A constable was sent to call
And found two windows shattered,
The first of which was spewing smoke.
Screams echoed through the latter.

No one survived.
They'd lost their lives
Together, washed in sorrow.
Their hands and feet tied by the thief
Who'd robbed them of tomorrow.
The next day brought a messenger
With tidings for consignment:
"Unless you wish to die as well,
You'll find a new assignment."

A paper note
With single fold,
Both ruled and perforated.
The ink, a dark blue water-based,
Was knuckle-rubbed and faded.
The penmanship: professional,

With perfect letter spacing.
Suggesting an expensive school
And years of letter tracing.

The left-handed
Aristocrat
Had gifted more than warning.
The letter had been handed off
Down by the docks that morning.
The giver was a haggard sort,
His beard both long and knotted.
His rags were soiled, his scent was sharp.
His shoes, though, were unspotted.

This charlatan,
A prideful man
Accustomed to deception,
Had waddled off, but never past
The depth of his perception.
Once satisfied he'd caused alarm,
He sank into an alley,
Resurfacing as someone new
To take a second tally.

A moment passed
That felt like days.
I spent the time surmising:
A face no one would recognize
Would not be worth disguising.
The changing man then disappeared

Into a carriage hollow,
L.A., of course, had seen him, too,
And signaled we should follow.

This carriage, large
And cumbersome,
Was forced to slow while turning
And would have lost its balance with
A driver less discerning.
The carriage kept to wider streets
(The path of least resistance).
We trailed on foot the cautious way:
In shadows at a distance.

The horses stopped
Outside a home
More aptly called a mansion.
The city seemed to sag under
The weight of its expansions.
The cobbled concave cul-de-sac
That crowned the gaslit terrace
Was burdened by two other homes,
Each equally as garish.

The driver helped
The man with bags
And boxes of all sizes
(Most certainly a gallery
Of all the rogue's disguises),
Then bowed the low, respectful bow

Reserved for men of station,
Extending forth an open palm
In search of compensation.

Once aptly paid,
And tipped as well,
The driver calmed his horses
Who'd stamped their hooves impatiently,
Each sensing evil forces.
Then darkness swallowed up the sight,
And soon the sound, of trotting.
We followed, satisfied we'd found
A starting point for plotting.

III.

The architect
Who built the home
Had never stopped designing.
He'd built two more and called them wings,
Intending to combine them.
And in these wings, with sundry lives,
Lived Widows Fern and Browning
Who'd lost their husbands years apart
To heart attack and drowning.

The middle home,
With massive size,
Was also mostly hollow.
From room to room a woman went.
The maids and butler followed.
Each day a man left and returned
(The beggar, we were certain).
All afternoon strange silhouettes
Were cast upon the curtains.

These shadow shapes,
By servants made,
Kept spreading then converging.
They gathered by the door each day to
Watch the man emerging.
Then back up to the woman's room

To sweep her past the dormer.
And on into another room,
And back into the former.

This dance played out
The same each day,
A cycle never ending.
The owner of the home was not
The only one pretending.
For days we watched this strange ballet,
Uncertain of its meaning.
Recording all that we observed
For any clue worth gleaning.

L.A. and I
Both held out hope
For other paths worth chasing.
We'd take any advantage with
No clue what we were facing.
Without another murder scene,
The papers wouldn't need us.
Thus, to the city registers
We let perception lead us.

Sir Brandon Blind
Had married young
For children and position.
His wife, though, bore him not one gift
By means of parturition.
The dowry he received, it seems,

Was apt to make one purchase:
A house sized right to hide his wife
That she may never surface.

Her father died
The day she wed,
Her mother long before him.
Which left her with a husband and
Nobody to adore him.
The house was sold for quite the sum.
The servants she was fond of
Had moved with her to her new home
To help her beat despondence.

An article
From near that time
Called loneliness her lover.
Another said she'd married well.
The Post called him her brother.
They all agreed she'd said farewell
To life as she had known it
And gained a life of solitude
With gossip as a bonus.

Sir Brandon Blind
Had changed as well.
Once quite the odd inventor,
He'd traded lenses, cogs and knobs
For buildings bankers enter.
Progress and knowledge suddenly

Meant less than coins and credits.
His patents had all gone unfiled
(Suspended pending edits).

IV.

New London nights
Are never still.
She always ups the ante.
Two stabbings and a burglary,
All foiled by vigilantes.
A robbery in Surrey Park
Had yet gone unreported.
It fell to us to tell the truth
Or let The Post distort it.

In river towns
The rumors flow
Like sewers, lies, and liquor.
You stop one up, it overflows
To drown us all the quicker.
While on the way to Surrey Park,
We met a source untrusted
And told them that the steel resolve
To break this case had rusted.

A simple lie
On rumor wings,
Ubiquitous as pigeons,
With tendency to propagate
(No different from religion).
We set it free near Market Square,

A social destination,
And watched as introduction turned
Into an infestation.

In Surrey Park,
A constable
Was taking victim statements.
Though, most appeared to have been forced
Into participation.
We erred at once on caution's side
And interviewed bystanders
Who all recalled the daft affair,
Most with an air of candor.

A coachman's purse,
Brim-full with coin,
And left out unattended
Had been snatched by a group of kids
And gleefully upended.
The frightened horses each escaped
(more stress than they could cope with).
Not satisfied, the kids made off
With ledger, hat, and coachwhip.

The coin cascade
Weighed down the walk
And pockets shortly after.
And all around the park there rang
The sound of children's laughter.
Three constables had been nearby

One chased the troublemakers,
The others gathered all in reach
To shame the money takers.

Fresh from the chase,
With flush-red face,
A tired lawman trotted.
He held the coachman's hat and whip,
The book he hadn't spotted
The ledger, we insisted, was
The primary objective.
The constable, with breathless voice,
Said "Wait for a detective."

We couldn't wait,
The coachman's face
Was one that we remembered.
This jarvey and his carriage wide
Had chauffeured the pretender.
The names, he said, were always writ,
With weights, if he was able,
And length of trip, to keep track of
Equine health at the stables.

A stablehand
Would meet him there
On Mondays and on Fridays
To copy down the ledger marks
And keep the records bi-ways.
Two records had been ledgerbound

And not yet duplicated,
But those had both been empty runs.
No passengers had made it.

A horse's coat,
If left unbrushed,
Will lead to irritation.
The hooves, as well, require care
To aid with ambulation.
A proper grooming helps a horse
Relieve both stress and tension.
It helps blood flow to muscles, too,
For injury prevention.

These facts we learned
At hurried pace
Through Market Square at sunset.
The ledger taken had no names,
The killer wasn't done yet.
Perhaps to speed us on our way,
Perhaps in search of vengeance,
The driver guided us up to,
And through, the stable entrance.

Nine empty stalls
Where normally
Nine horses would be waiting
Gave focus to the tenth, in which
A tiny life was fading.
A hooded figure near the rear

Set fire to a haystack.
We grabbed the stableboy and fled,
The driver vowing payback.

The fire raged
Throughout the day
Then turned to ash and embers.
The shadow of a man was all
The poor boy could remember.
The ledger, we were sure, was gone,
Or eaten by the fire.
The only clue remaining was
The arsonist's attire.

V.

The hooded cloak
Was black as night,
With buttons at the shoulders,
And would have seemed less out of place
If it were somewhat colder.
The buttons were the polished sort,
Made from a yellow metal,
Just like those seen on Broker Road,
Where bank disputes are settled.

New London streets
Had gone to calm
Save horses not yet captured.
Few had been found, and some put down
For madness and for fractures.
The vigilantes prowled at night.
The constables ignored them.
The carriages grew lonesome, too,
With nobody to board them.

On Broker Road
The overcoats
And cloaks were all in season.
With summer tones and collar points
And cape lengths within reason.
Though some had been adorned with stars

Or suns or moons in crescents,
For anyone with worth to claim
The buttons, too, were present.

This symbol of
Fraternity
Came with a code of silence.
A member had to wear them both
To keep within compliance.
As all or none of them could be
The killer, we were wary.
A bearer of the buttons, though,
Approached with commentary.

The news, he said,
Could do with more
On New London's finances.
He spoke as though he did not see
His fellow banker's glances.
When bumped into quite forcefully
He stumbled into knowing.
Then gathered his composure and
Suggested we be going.

We left at once,
Though showed no haste,
More furious than frightened.
We'd both been threatened many times.
The noose had never tightened.
We walked along through shaded streets

With footfalls trailing tightly,
Confirmed the tail with turns, and then
Confronted them, politely.

Sir Brandon Blind
We came to find
Accountable for stalking.
Instead of fessing to the deed
He simply said "Keep Walking."
We crossed the street at once so that
We'd not be seen together.
Then followed as if pulled along
By lengthy, hidden tethers.

Arriving at
His mansion home
He gestured to the pleasance.
We waited while he went inside
Then scanned for others present.
Surveillance of this grand estate
Worked best from certain places.
We checked each of them, one by one.
Twice over in some cases.

When it was clear
We weren't watched
We shuffled past the roses
And entered through the pantry door
While striking servants poses.
The maids and butler ushered us

To where their master waited.
Three chairs around a table sat.
Three lunches had been plated.

The centerpiece,
A spread of fruit,
Was lush, and fully ripened.
A treat that we could scarce afford
On journalism stipends.
The tableware was rimmed in gold.
The cloches were designer.
The tablecloth was pure white silk.
I'd never seen one finer.

And dressed just as
Sir Blind had been,
Though obviously smaller,
A woman stood on foot-high stilts
Designed to make her taller.
In fact, if not for how she stood
We never would have seen them,
Distracted by the pair of maids
That knelt down in-between them.

Two others stood
On either side
To aid with stabilizing
While straps were carefully undone.
A stance most compromising.
A maid ran in with acetone

(despite herself she spilled some)
And dabbed at tiny specks of glue
Stuck to the woman's philtrum.

We watched in awe
As Brandon Blind
Was cast off like attire.
And in his place stood Susan Blind,
Her brown eyes full of fire.
The butler pulled out all three chairs
And tucked them in beneath us.
We sat and heard the tale and tasks
The Lady Blind bequeathed us.

VI.

Young Brandon Blind
And Suzy Fane
Had always loved each other.
They met when they were very young.
They'd both just lost their mothers.
When Brandon's father passed as well,
Sir Fane filed for adoption
And raised young Brandon like a son
(For lack of better options).

Sir Enwood Fane
Gained wealth and name
From father and grandfather.
They each had worn the Two Moons cloak,
But Enwood didn't bother.
The name, he felt, bore weight enough
To anchor his ambitions.
The Order of the Cosmos, though,
Insisted on tradition.

Insist, they did,
On many things,
With vinegar, not honey.
And in return Sir Enwood Fane
Gained providence and money.
He strayed but once before his death,

Rejecting their pretenses,
And lost his wife that very day.
A game of consequences.

The rules now known,
He wrote his own.
Two games would play in concert.
The Order knew of Susan Fane.
He couldn't just ensconce her.
Instead he taught her all he knew,
Intent on her protection,
While doing as The Order bid.
A game of misdirection.

The girl grew smart,
Both street and book,
And skilled at infiltration.
Meanwhile, her father rose in ranks
To Duke of Constellations.
The Two Moons cloak had gained much sway
But gained more burden with it.
One day The Order asked too much
And Enwood wouldn't give it.

The value of
The Fane estate,
And blood, had risen steeply.
By then his ward and daughters hearts
Were intertwined too deeply.
A plan to wed the Half Eclipse

And Two Moons was abandoned
When Enwood Fane the Third said no
And Susan married Brandon.

They waited for
Her wedding day
Then showed up uninvited,
Surprising not one person there.
The Fanes had been farsighted.
The Constellation King and Lords
Were given premiere seating,
And pointed out as honored guests
When invitees were eating.

They left before
Dessert was served
This, too, had been expected.
Amongst his friends and family,
Sir Fane was well protected.
Since weddings only last so long,
He knew his hours numbered.
Still, planning one's death in advance
Does leave you unencumbered.

He danced and drank.
He danced some more.
He bade farewells and blisses.
He gave a toast to future Blinds
Birthed to Mister and Missus.
He'd led a life of triumph with

So very few exceptions,
And not only saw Susan wed,
But lived through the reception.

Thus, Enwood Fane
Was well and done
When chaos came to find him.
The bride and groom had slipped away,
The guests not far behind them.
He took a dining chair and sat
Beside a dying fire.
His shoulders sagged beneath the cloak,
His funeral attire.

The moonlight white
Was overshone
By yellow from a candle
That glowed inside a lantern's cage
With no apparent handle.
The lantern flew into the room.
For this, Sir Fane had waited.
The lantern shot a beam of light.
Sir Fane asphyxiated.

Sir Fane the Third,
Was torn in two,
His soul and body fractured.
The beam spread wide, engulfed the room.
Poor Enwood's soul was captured.
The light had cut through space and time,

A cosmic laceration,
And partly through Sir Brandon Blind
In search of rehydration.

Its quarry caught,
The lantern left,
And moonlight filled the hallway.
Sir Blind could feel a change in him.
He'd died, but in a small way.
When Susan rose the morning next,
Aglow from fete and sleeping,
She saw two bodies still and cold,
And heard her husband weeping.

VII.

Had we not seen
The things we'd seen,
Her words would have spurred laughter.
Instead we sat like monoliths
Throughout the tale and after.
The servants had been watching us
To gauge any reaction.
They saw what they had hoped to see
And shuffled into action.

With rational,
Interpretive,
And scientific thinking,
L.A. and I had courted death
As journalists, unblinking.
Now all the things we thought were real
Were subject to suspicion.
The truths we knew could all be false,
Facts could be superstition.

The time to think
Through all these thoughts
Was minuscule and fleeting.
The servants cleared away the food
That no one had been eating.
The butler cleared his throat and then

Announced the ghost of Brandon.
The servants cleared the room in fear.
Decorum was abandoned.

The facts had changed.
Before us stood
A brand new understanding.
The Phantom Blind was there and not,
Contracting and expanding.
Like smoke inside of sculpted glass,
Vicissitude assembled,
It looked at us through half-there eyes
And when it spoke, we trembled.

"My body rots.
My conscience fades:
The half-life of a specter.
My only hope is in the light.
The lantern soul collector."
The form then swirled as if exhaled,
We noticed a resemblance
The Phantom Blind appeared to be
The ghost that stole remembrance.

The shade reshaped,
Or nearly so,
Its voice was strained and shaking.
"We need your help in tracking down
The tool of my unmaking."
It faded as if it had used

The time it was allotted.
A maid who entered far too soon
Screamed once and then forgot it.

Perhaps to think,
Perhaps to find
Some purchase (we were reeling),
L.A. and I excused ourselves,
In dire need of steeling.
We walked towards the garden door,
Intent on rumination.
Instead we turned and faced the truth,
Much to the maid's elation.

The Lady Blind
Was pleased as well,
Beneath her disposition.
She nodded to us passively,
Her plan nearing fruition.
"You've chosen well, the both of you.
Exactly as expected.
You've no doubt realized we three
Alone are unaffected."

"The only ones,
From what I've seen,
Who can remember Brandon
When he has come and gone again
With revenant abandon."
The maid beside her hung her head,

Assuming recent failings,
Then reddened slightly from the shame
And hid her face, exhaling.

"New London thinks
My husband lives,
Thus, only we can help him."
While Susan spoke, she rang a bell
To bring the other help in.
The butler brought with him a map
And laid it on the table.
It showed New London's Northern edge,
From Docktown to the stables.

Three crosses marked
Three places where
The lantern could be hidden.
Three banks that called to Brandon's soul,
Where strangers were forbidden.
The Order of the Cosmos owned
Most New London resources,
But neutral parties owned the North,
The Docklands, and the horses.

The archives held
No records that
Could justify what lay there.
The banks were wildly out of place
The Order had no sway there.
And, though they called to Brandon's soul,

The soul could never enter.
Like shadows pressed back by the light
Deep in the lantern's center.

The soul did search,
Many a night,
Drawn to the lantern's victims.
'Salvation waits inside the light'
The phantom's latest dictum.
And, though it found a body and
A widow on arrival,
It never made it there in time
To kindle its revival.

We spoke with it
When time allowed.
The pain was clearly growing.
The shape it took was less defined
With each coming and going.
Without the light, the lovers Blind
Had no hope for returning
To normalcy, to life, to love.
A future most concerning.

L.A. and I
Both hoped to find
The lantern and destroy it.
A plan we knew may not comply
With motives to employ it.
The Blinds had tried to warn us off,

And then in us confided.
We'd help them use the lantern first,
Then snuff the light inside it.

VIII.

We strategized
At frantic pace.
The Phantom Blind was waning.
With it would fade the tattered shreds
Of hope that were remaining.
It taught us all about the banks,
At least from its perspective:
A specter no one could recall.
The phantom's retrospective.

The Order's banks
Were guarded well
By armed, attentive sentries
Who let through only certain men.
The pins were key to entry.
All loiterers and passersby
Would face intimidation,
And constables were kept at bay
By means of exploitation.

The buildings had
But one door each,
No windows were detected.
No mail came for delivery,
No waste ever collected.
Only The Order came and went,

Though, seemingly at random,
And always just one man alone,
No triplicates or tandems.

Three women, then,
Would enter banks
Across town as three men would.
All standing tall and wearing proud
The cloaks and pins of Enwood.
With confidence, and in disguise,
Each searcher would be wary
Of people who could recognize
The pins that we were wearing.

The wayward soul
Of Brandon Blind
Would wait for us in hiding
And come back when we called from where
The lantern was residing.
A perfect plan it could not be
Too much was too well hidden.
Not one of us knew what we'd find
When we arrived unbidden.

I modified
My cloak to fit
The items I was bringing.
The Order never carried bags,
Their hands were busy wringing.
A stick of chalk, a water flask,

A tiny torch and matches:
The sum of all that I could fit
In pockets made of patches.

Susan assigned,
By random choice,
The banks that we would enter.
I took the West, L.A. the East,
And Susan took the center.
The ingress times were synchronized
With dusk to match the gloaming,
When day was gray just like the mood
And not a soul was roaming.

I walked into
A lobby made
Of glass with gold adornments.
A guard was sleeping in his chair.
The teller, too, lay dormant.
The walls echoed the sounds of steps
But didn't wake the sleepers.
Two others walked into the hall:
My fellow secret keepers.

A stream of light
From overhead
Illuminated faces
That should have been some blocks away,
In independent places.
The three of us, identical,

In Enwood Fane disguises,
Snuck through the hall before the guard
Could wake and scrutinize us.

This time we used
A single door,
In single file, enraptured.
More focused on the strangeness than
The chance we could be captured.
L.A. and Susan led the way.
I closed the door behind us,
Then marked it with a piece of chalk
In hopes it would remind us.

A maze of doors
Led back and forth
Through hallways long and twisted.
I marked each one that we might find
The way back unassisted.
And when we three had walked so far
That all six feet were aching,
We came upon a door that held
The chalk marks I'd been making.

All thirty marks
(I'd kept a count),
Exactly where I'd placed them,
In graduating altitudes,
As though someone had traced them.
Exhaustion, yes, and anger, too,

But mostly base confusion
Engulfed my mind. We had to find
An end to this illusion.

IX.

We stopped to think
And leaned against
The doorway with my markings.
To calm the nerves and formulate
A plan before embarking.
The dim light cast upon the walls
Revealed a shallow etching
That one could see when very close.
These shadows needed stretching.

The tiny torch
I'd filled with oil
And capped with cork for travel.
The braided cotton wick was soaked.
I let the end unravel.
I struck a match and lit the torch.
Its light was long and narrow.
I held the torch up to the wall.
The shadows stretched to arrows.

The arrows lead
In what seemed like
A circle, though we followed.
I passed around my water flask
Each tiny drop was swallowed.
We came upon a door that looked

Exactly like the others,
But only here did arrows meet
And point to one another.

This newfound door
We let swing wide
And looked before encroaching.
The torch had dimmed to some degree
Its end was soon approaching.
We stepped into the roundish room
The doorway closed behind us,
The flicker of the tiny torch
The sole relief from blindness.

In widened arc
I painted light
Across the pitch black setting.
With bodies begging for a rest
And lips in need of wetting,
We stumbled slowly through the room,
Not sure where we were going.
Just as we reached the centerpoint,
The lantern started glowing.

The torch went out
For lack of oil,
So little was remaining.
The lantern rose. The torch relit.
It burned on, self-sustaining.
The lantern flew away from us

Towards the wall behind it.
It fired out a beam of light.
The three of us were blinded.

I rubbed my eyes
And looked about
Through tears and blurry vision.
The light had cut a window out
With surgical precision.
The Lady Blind
Stepped in its path.
Her prey would not escape her.
The lantern shot another beam.
It cut through her like paper.

Body and soul
Stood side by side
No longer than a shudder.
The lantern flew between the two.
They stared at one another.
The body fell, the soul exhaled,
Now Susan Blind: Unbounded.
I passed my torchlight over it
And skin grew back around it.

With shrieks of pain
The Lady Blind
Was reincorporated.
And as she was the corpse she left
Dimmed like a torch then faded.

Once Susan was herself again
She called out to her lover,
Who was not more than mist by then.
It hovered just above her.

I raised the light
To heal the mist
But caused no transformation.
The Blind Divide had been, perhaps,
Too long a separation.
"The lantern is the only way.
It holds the purest power,"
The mist cried out in Brandon's voice,
"I'll fade within the hour."

Into the clothes
She'd worn before
The brand new Susan scurried.
The lantern could be on its way.
She knew we had to hurry.
The torch, placed on the lantern's stand,
Was pointed at the window.
The lantern would be forced to glow,
Thus, ending Brandon's limbo.

X.

That none had come
To find us here
I found all too concerning.
Someone had sent the lantern out,
Knew when it was returning.
The hallway just beyond the door
Was etched with indicators
That someone else could follow to
This room full of invaders.

L.A. agreed
To guard the door.
I probed the lantern's egress.
Though it was wide enough for us,
The fall was long and treeless.
With eyes adjusting to the dark
And torchlight aiding slightly,
I tied the cloaks and costume pants
Together, lengthwise, tightly.

The makeshift rope
Relied on seams
Sewn by New London's tailors.
With sturdy stitching favored by
Ship captains and their sailors.
The cloaks and pants were made of silk,

A soft thread good for dyeing.
The cloth was tight, but stretched a bit,
Which made it good for tying.

We checked once more
Beyond the door,
Heard footsteps in the distance.
The mist took form one final time
Against Susan's insistence.
We waited for a magic light
In darkness, as if dreaming.
The ghost of Brandon left the room.
The hallway filled with screaming.

A hand forgot,
A torch was dropped,
The maze was filled with fire.
The ghost returned with smoke in tow.
The screaming man expired.
The burning flames devoured air.
A vacuum was created.
The door slammed shut, protecting us
From chaos while we waited.

The sound of bells
And sirens, too,
Came ringing through the city.
The Docklands burned again tonight.
We had no time for pity.
The fire raged ten blocks away,

But also fifteen paces.
And by the time the dawn arrived,
Ash would replace both places.

I tied the rope
Around the stand
The lantern would return to,
While hoping that the fire would
Have better doors to burn through.
I hung the rope to test its length
(Quick deaths would come from stalling).
It reached ten feet above the ground.
We'd reach the rest by falling.

Over the roofs
A yellow glow
Was headed right towards us.
The lantern had allotted all
The time it could afford us.
Whoever it was sent to find
It found and, no doubt ended.
A brand-new body river bound,
A new soul apprehended.

The mist was weak,
Seemed spread too far.
Smoke crept in, giving warning:
We had to bring him back at once.
There'd be no time for mourning.
The lantern flew into the room,

Back from its sordid mission.
The torchlight met the lantern first.
It glowed in recognition.

The lantern glowed
A quaint response.
The mist cried out in anguish.
The door erupted into flames.
The light began to languish.
Some strength returned; the mist took form.
The lantern light responded.
In agony, Sir Brandon's soul
And body were re-bonded.

The fire left
The labyrinth
And crawled along the ceiling.
The lantern filled the room with light
And Brandon finished healing.
L.A. sent Susan down the rope
Then she and Brandon followed.
I grabbed my torch and scaled the wall
Just as the room was swallowed.

XI.

An amber night,
Lit both by moon
And by the light of fires,
Illuminated four lost souls
In scandalous attire.
I hadn't reached the ground in time,
Fell longer than intended.
The torch shone on my fractured leg.
My leg was fully mended.

The torch went dim,
A dying light,
Igniting hopes for closure.
It flickered then went dark at last,
No flame in its enclosure.
Some garments from the rope remained.
By four they were divided.
A passing horse expressed distaste.
Its neighs went unrequited.

We walked along
Through smoke-filled streets
Together, nearly broken.
Companions in an anxious place
Where not a word was spoken,
Then parted ways at Market Square,

The North and South divider,
And bade farewell with solemn nods
Confider to confider.

Hot summer days.
Cool in the shade.
Warm ash in need of wetting.
No longer would the streets be plagued
By phantoms and forgetting.
The Order felt a loss that night:
A great deal of their power.
They'd stay the same, but we had changed.
The greatest loss was ours.

We'd found the truth
As we had vowed,
Though lies would suit us better.
The truth would both be disbelieved
And see us thrown in fetters.
The Blinds agreed to do their part
To see the lie delivered.
The rains came down and washed the ash
Away into the river.

The scavengers
Picked at the sites,
Exploring ever deeper.
They found no hidden mazes there,
No lantern, nor its keeper.
I've kept the torch all of these years,

A souvenir worth fearing.
Should ever it take flame again
I'll know the lantern's nearing.

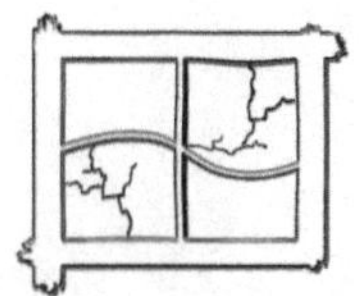

NURSE LUCY

My soul is on the edge of insanity,
My eyes dilated and red.
Death threats and fairy tales flow through my mind
As I lay here strapped to the bed.
I can hear the men speaking,
The floor creaking.
They walk into the next room instead
Because they know in their hearts
That my life ends and starts
With the death threats that run through my head.

Insanity is here with me I can hear breathing or is that my breath?
Insanity won't let me be and I fear that she is all I have left.

I am afraid of what dreams can make of me
As they dance along behind my eyes.
Life is a joke, but nobody's laughing.
You hear the punchline when you die.
I can feel my soul fading,
My mind wading

Through the truths that I've told with my lies.
And I could never explain
How my head aches with pain
When the death threats careen through my mind.

Insanity is here with me I can hear breathing or is that my breath?
Insanity won't let me be and I fear that she is all I have left.

It is time for my bi-weekly counseling.
They unstrap me and lead me away.
The echoing moans of men circle me.
They're not well and so here they must stay.
In my head I hear one thought:
Kill them or not?
It's a game that we all one day play.
With my decision now found,
They lay still on the ground
As my vision once more turns to gray.

Insanity is here with me I can hear breathing or is that my breath?
Insanity won't let me be and I fear that she is all I have left.

I awake with guards surrounding me.
They are angry, they will me much pain.
A nurse kindly cleans blood from my hands
And she whispers, 'You're completely sane'.
I can feel the gray coming,
My mind numbing.
She buries my psyche in sand.
When I wake from the shot

I'll be back on my cot
Singing death threats no one understands.

Insanity is here with me I can hear breathing or is that my breath?
Insanity won't let me be and I fear that she is all I have left.

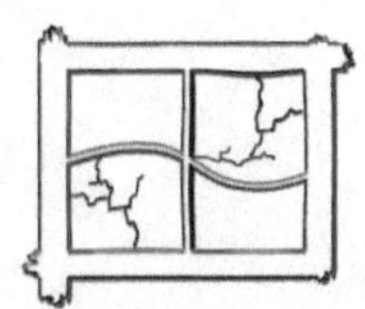

L'Amour

Her cigarette ash
Stained fingers can dash,
Like lights,
Over, under cash.
Counts it in a flash
Each night.
To pinch for her stash
She has to be brash,
In sight.

The faster the eye
The more it can spy,
It seems.
A Pinkerton guy
Here hopes to descry
The scheme.
He's welcome to try.
She'll simply deny.
Esteem

Has swollen her pride.
It's harder to hide
These days.
No one to confide
In makes her abide
Some grays.
Yet still dignified.
Fights taken outside,
Liaised.

That Pinkerton man
Is hatching a plan,
And yet,
A stud poker fan.
He'll win if he can.
His bet
Was dead in the pan
Before he began.
Upset.

Lost money to grieve.
No way to retrieve.
He sighs.
A flick of a sleeve.
He does not believe
His eyes.
Two aces retrieved
From slow witted thieves
The prize.

The Madame returns
From outside to learn
The news.
A Pinkerton spurned.
No cause for concern.
Amused.
The agent is stern.
Demands what was earned.
Refused.

A scene to be made.
The threat of a raid
Clears out
Her good clientèle.
"You're leaving as well,"
She shouts.
The Pinkerton preens,
Says something obscene,
And flouts.

The Madame plays cool.
She knows well the rules
In play.
Can't kill him inside,
But can't let him ride
Away.
The second he's out
She kills him without
Delay.

Her reputation,
As well as station
In town.
Are rooted too deep.
The queen gets to keep
Her crown.
Knows her day will come.
'Til then she's of some
Renown.

Come one and come all,
Short, fat, skinny, tall,
And more.
For whiskey and games,
For music and dames
Galore.
Just try not to cross
The Madame, the boss,
L'Amour.

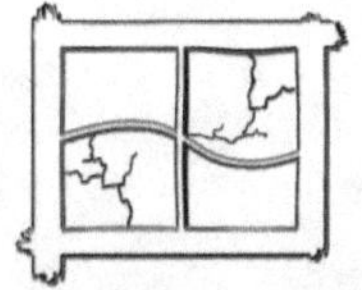

I Cry When I Laugh

Something simple, somehow shocking
Laughable, I'm losing life
Left for dead after they shot me
Bullets broke the air in flight
Led each other to my bloodstream
Went so deep, they holed my soul
Sharp like glass with heat like sunbeams
Definitely took a toll

Never understood existence
Laughable, I'm losing life
Dying, living, what's the difference
Bought the bullet, paid the price
Gentlemen that shot me down took
Little over twenty cents
Pride held tight my wallet, now look
Down the drain my life just went

Over, under, leaning, laying
Laughable, I'm losing life

Stole away without delaying
Pitter-patters in the night
Wonder how long I will live now
That my body's torn apart
Feel my mind, it wants to give out
Same condition as my heart

Pain is real, asphalt I'm groping
Laughable, I'm losing life
Like the blood on which I'm choking
Inner wounds are out of sight
Blood internal, world receding
Soul retreating from this Earth
C'mon, heart, just keep on beating
Body's numb, it doesn't hurt

Hope the paramedics hurry
Laughable, I'm losing life
Tears ran out, my eyes are blurry
Can't give up, I've got to fight
There's a siren in the distance
Pain cuts through me like a knife
Something simple, somehow shocking
Laughable, I've lost my life

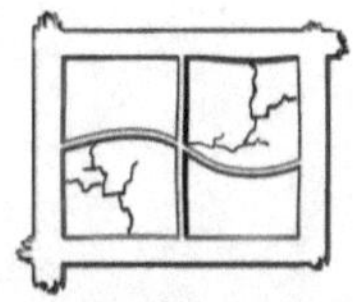

STEEL SOUL

Time has no use for me.
I drift in a starry sea.
What ails me most, robotics just,
Is
I can never truly live.

By this I mean to dream.
Metal's what went into me.
And solitude, and man-made rules.
Script
Of the monologue I give.

Who is going to play to me
When all in life is done?
No need for prayer, I am not real
I won't rot, rust will come.

If not for bitter circumstance, I'd pull out my wires.
I'm made to smile and made to see this life as hellish fires.
And still my program keeps me so damned happy.

I'd sleep it off if only I were programmed to be tired.

Red eyes, no vision, just recordings played real-time.
Your heart can beat, it's sad – I hum to life, feel mine.
And feel as well how cold I am- like my thoughts.
That is, of course, assuming I've a mind.

Who is going to play to me
When all in life is done?
No need for prayer, I am not real
I won't rot, rust will come.

I know of Dorothy, and Scarecrow, oh, and of the Lion.
I also know of no one 'round who doesn't plan on dyin'.
No need for tears or I'll rust right here.
Of that truth there's no denyin'.

Time, it's got its hold on me.
It's beautiful, I'm ugly- this is the only life I see.
But what ails me so, robotics just,
Is that I cannot believe.

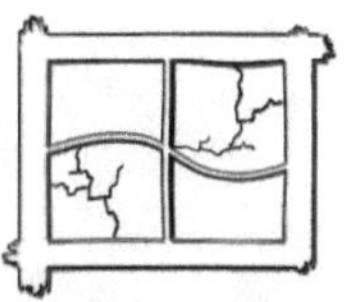

FIT

I Need to put on my skin,
but I have no way in.
The eye holes are way too small.
The mouth can get wide and can fit me inside,
But, look,
I can't close it at all.
The legs are all floppy.
I don't think it fits.
The bottom's all toppy.
Is this where I sit?
I can't find the elbows.
I stretched out the chin.
The color is perfect, but is this my skin?

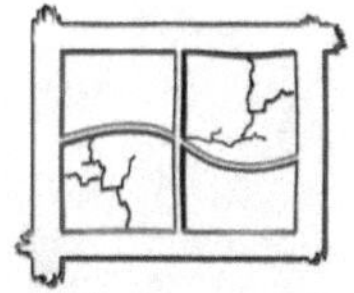

RIVERSIDER

Way, way, down along the riverside
I found my boat and sailed away
The river was coarse; the course was hard
It was hard to ward off my watery grave

Way, way down I sailed the river wide
A lonely soul on a bed of foam
Alone I'll stay until I find my way
To that place back home to which I roam

Take; take me down to where this river ends
And spill me out into the sea
The jungles I pass are full of eyes
That not only look; but reach for me

Take; take me now, I just can't take no more
If this river wins, I'll lose my soul
The waters blue, the waters crystal clear
They're pulling me in, these waters cold

I know I need to go away,
Away, away, a – wait a minute, now
I know I need to go away
But it's so hard to do; I know it now
I know I need to go away
Away, away, way...

Way, way, down along the riverside
I docked my boat and walked ashore
The river had soaked me right down to the bone
My clothes were ruined; my heart was torn

Way, way down I felt a pain inside
As I walked this road to darker days
The road was rough, and though my eyes were dry
I tried to cry my fears away

Take; take me down to where the crossroads meet
So I can sit and die awhile
Take; take me now, this is my destiny
I've known it since I was a child

I know I need to go away,
Away, away, a – wait a minute, now
I know I need to go away
But it's so hard to do; I know it now
I know I need to go away
Away, away, way...

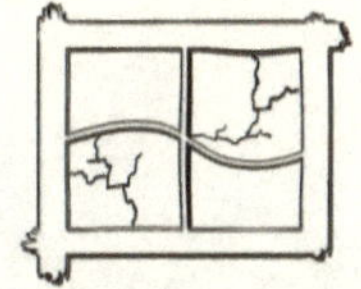

SMOKE IN HER MIRROR

Giraffes in the garden
Made of rose, all made in rows
Punk princess, incensed with being here
Cigarettes she smokes
Guitars of glass hardened
By time and a breeze of cold
Angry girl, calls them ashtrays
Wish she didn't smoke

You want to ruin me, she says
As she ruins all she touches
Midas feeling in the dark
Towards ignorance she rushes

Guilty, never pardoned
As she leaves our anger goes
Punk princess, upset that she was here
Match paper she folds
About love she's ardent
Yet she burns the world she knows

Angry girl, your world's aflame
Wish you didn't smoke

You'll never ruin me, she cries
As she spoils all she touches
Midas feeling in the dark
Towards ignorance she rushes

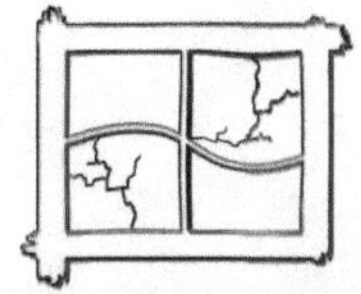

TRAINWRECK

I'm handling abandoning virtue pretty well.

Have a picture of my Heaven, though I don't believe in Hell.

Unconscious dreams of a monstrous me

Keep me tense, as though I'm under a spell.

RELAXING

My life is fine, so what if I'm the epitome of insanity?

With so many minds behind two eyes, I do what they demand of me.

I've no disguise to hide behind

Except the man I plan to be.

MINDTRAP

Trains don't give a smooth ride, and it's hard as shit to write.

I guess it doesn't help that we're careening through the night.

I'm pretty sure both conductors

Just came asking for a light.

SMOKER'S CONCERN

I'm choking on the smoke coming from the engine room.

First the tickets, then the luggage, then the ride, and then the doom.

And I just had to read that magazine

That said, my life was ending soon.

HOROSCOPES

Shouldn't there be an emergency brake hanging on the wall?
Tried running down the fucking aisle but can't seem not to fall.
This emergency phone doesn't have a dial tone.
It's okay; it's too late to make the call.
HEAD RINGING?

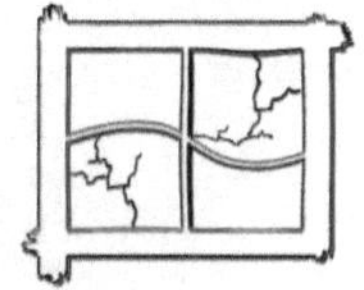

SUNSTORMER

As yellow turned to orange, we all foresaw the gray.
Street lanterns quickly lighted (in hopes to stretch the day).
The night is heavy, leans on sunshine, hides it all away.
The burning ball of gas put on one final grand display
Then sputtered out and left us all in darkness.

"Whoever has the courage must go relight the sun."
The Mayor didn't offer (he had a town to run).
This burden's heavy, not something he'd put on anyone,
But panic had been spreading since the darkness had begun,
So someone had to volunteer regardless.

A dozen men stepped forward, twice that in women brave.
The danger didn't matter. They had a world to save.
Their hearts were heavy, full of sadness. Peace was what they craved.
They stood through the remainder of the speech the mayor gave
Then left to learn the rules to flying rockets.

There was no time for lessons. They skipped straight to the tests.
There were no second chances, nor study time, nor rest.

The suits were heavy, most complained of pressure on their chests.
Of thirty-six, the engineers felt only two impressed
(The ones with good luck charms stuffed in their pockets).

The lucky two weren't lazy, they pitched in where they could,
Then practiced poking buttons (as spaceship pilots should).
The mood was lightened, now the task was fully understood.
The optimism spread through town like fire through the woods,
But hope hides many dangers in the darkness.

Three shuttles had been crafted. Each built with rockets, two.
Each rocket had three stages with times the pilots knew.
The sun, once lighted, would be hot, their math had to be true.
They couldn't just fly close enough, they had to fly right through
And jettison a rocket where the heart is.

The third shuttle would wait there (in case the first two failed).
A board was placed before it. To it a sign was nailed.
"We'd be delighted if this spaceship never had to sail."
The pilots took their places, rockets waiting to exhale,
When suddenly a storm rolled in around them.

The clouds marched in with thunder, erasing all the stars.
The pilots lifted off into a sky as black as tar.
Avoiding lightning fingers reaching for them from afar,
They cut straight through the darkness leaving two emblazoned scars
And marveled at where fickle fate had found them.

Around them other rockets were cutting through the clouds.
So many soaring skyward made every pilot proud.

With streaks of fire following, up rose the rocket crowd.
To reach the sun and light is what each of them had vowed
While knowing they were likely not returning.

With pride comes satisfaction. With height, a blinking gauge.
The pilots checked their timing. They lit the second stage.
Most rockets fired, others though, would simply not engage.
Unable to escape, those pilots cursed their rocket cage
And plummeted with wings and bodies burning

The pilots still remaining shed tears but soldiered on.
They each had made a promise to reignite the dawn.
Their hearts afire, thoughts with loved ones, fear was all but gone.
They rose like voices to the stars they all had wished upon
And headed for the solar system's center.

In space there's room to ponder and doubt can stretch its wings.
The darkness and the silence, the fear they tend to bring,
Can spread like fire, all consuming, minds are fragile things.
One pilot turning back made many more start panicking.
They turned around to follow the dissenter.

All hope had not departed. Two pilots still remained.
Good luck charms in their pockets, conviction in their veins,
Their minds were steady. Turning back would teeter on insane.
Without the sun alight the darkness evermore would reign
And lamplight doesn't warm the soul like sunshine.

The second stage was ending, the window had been tight.
Towards the solar center they sputtered through the night.

Their speed was steady, buttons lit, objective in their sight.
They split for the approach (one from the left, one from the right),
Then charged in hard like soldiers on the front line.

They jettisoned their rockets, a stage each worth of fuel,
And braced for the explosion. Alas, fate can be cruel.
The dark instead of burning light meant they had all been fools.
The trip took far too long, the sun was given time to cool.
There was no secondary plan to light it.

A streak of desperation came burning through the black.
The cavalry of cowards had been seen turning back
And in their stead a small-town mayor launched the last attack.
He barreled past his neighbors to the solar cardiac
And felt the heat of pride as it ignited.

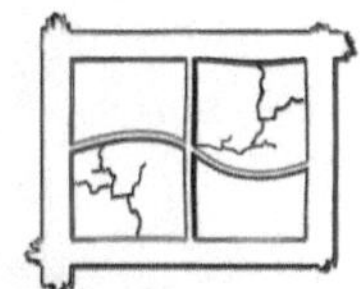

THE BLOWBACK

I once tried to leap from a cliff.
The wind would not allow it.
My mind said, "It's not when, but if."
Vowed it.

I tried to get a running start,
But ran in place, went nowhere.
I found I had no windproof parts.
Warfare.

I crawled, tip-toed, and even rolled.
My mind keeps senses heightened.
She thinks I've long-since lost control.
Frightened.

What chafes me most is not the wind
But what lies at its nether.
My mind said to have thicker skin.
Leather.

I leaned, I leaned, over the cliff.
The wind just gently turned me
And walked me back - a lovers' tiff.
Spurned me.

I heard the waves, saw gulls on high.
The vision was spellbinding.
The wind blew sand into my eyes.
Blinding.

I walked for days both East and West.
The cliff just never ended.
I left. The wind did not protest.
Splendid.

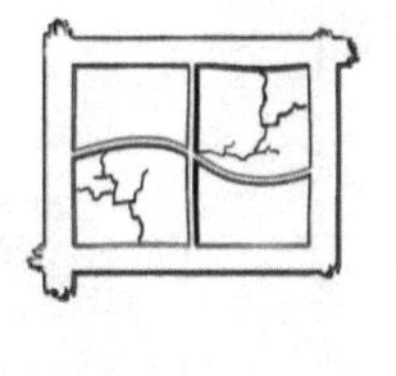

Snow

Snow
Like soft, white snow
She falls like snow
And then it happens
Almost like a madness
I fall deeply in love
To have to hold
And not just now, but all forever
Just as long as we're together
She's -

Snow
Like soft, white snow
She falls like snow
Against the mattress
I go tumbling after
Now we make, we're in love
She's all I know
And all i care to for that matter
While her belly's getting fatter
She's -

Snow
Like soft, white snow
She falls like snow
Into the laughter
Chasing pitter-patters
Tiny feet that we love
In time they grow
Just like the distance does between us
I'm a discontented dreamer
She's -

Snow
Like soft, white snow
She falls like snow
I try to catch her
She's not looking backwards
So I know that she's gone
She won't come home
This place is nothing but a house now
Turn the lights and cupboards out now
She's -

Snow
Like soft, white snow
She falls like snow
Forever after
All the mem'ries match with
All the reasons she's gone
That much I know

And what's more, now I understand
That she was never meant to handle
She's -

Snow
Like soft, white snow
And what's more, I must admit
That she was always delicate, yes,
She's Snow

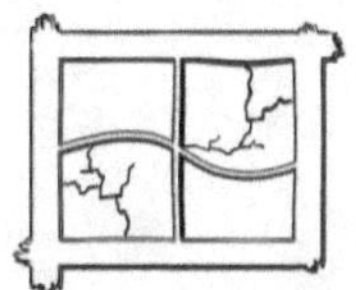

THAT SINKING FEELING

How can I suppress these chains upon my breath?
As I fall down from afloat, waters rise now in my chest.
I'd gasp out for air, but I know none is left.
Here in pain I remain: a fish forgotten in his death.

I dreamed I was drowning, now I've drowned. Am I dreaming?
As I lay in murky depths, the sun, too far above, is gleaming.
So cold, my body folds. I close my eyes, no use in screaming.
Found some coral, found a friend. On this reef I'm limp and leaning.

Oh, it's funny here in darkness, how you cannot hear a sound.
When you're floating in the water, you're not thinking of the ground.
My soul can swim, I'm sure, though to my body it is bound.
I'm King of Clowns. My teardrops, mixed with water, make my
crown.

Dear God, take me to Heaven. I don't think that I can wait.
These waters hold me lonely, though the slaves they helped escape.
I never went near water, bought a boat and met my fate.
Please forgive me if I'm soggy when I get to Heaven's gates.

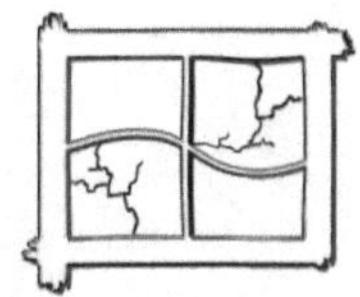

ARIDAMISSA

She'd watched them, from youth, day by day, from a rock in the bay that the waves let be.

The brave Tearterran peasant, Princess Kiralay, and Syrena, who watched from the sea.

They'd all grown up together, their ages the same, on the shores of the Tearterran isle.

Though the peasant loved one, he could never have known he was loved by two after a while.

Though she tried and she tried, she could not gain his eye, and she suffered in silence at sea.

While the love shared by princess and peasant grew real, she dreamed daily of how it could be.

Be damned this need.
There lies asleep a beast in me.
It's caged, but still
Upon my heart it loves to feed.
It seeks to leave its cage.

One day it will succeed.
My hope is that it will.

I cannot kill
This beast. It never has its fill.
Desire, greed,
My wants seep through walls I build.
I've tried to disengage,
Leave this beast unfulfilled,
I never do succeed.

And the Lurelish king by the name of Kitai, how he hated the poor island boy.

He would weep on his throne for he could not condone such a mate for his one pride and joy.

My will is weak, my words are weaker.
The men I rule remain the meeker.
They have no choice; the gods have spoken:
I'm king until my will be broken.
My Lureland, how I adore thee.
How I despise those poor unworthies
Who dance upon Tearterran beaches,
And dive beyond my minions' reaches,
For these such men have caused to me
Much time spent pondering my grief.

Though their love he forbade, he still let Kiralay spend her days on the Tearterran sands.

All the while in his head hung the hope she would wed to a prince from a faraway land.

And there came such a day when a young Kiralay told Kitai that she'd fallen in love.

Celebration ensued. Kitai never perused who it was that his daughter spoke of.

When the wedding month came, Kiralay gave the name of the suitor who'd stolen her heart.

When Kitai heard the news, he was sad and confused, wanting only to keep them apart.

You've always known I'd love him
Why are you surprised?
Why fight it?

On deaf ears fell his pleas, and he fell to his knees, but his daughter would not change her mind.

So, from high on his throne Kitai sat all alone, growing angrier, hostile, unkind.

While he ate fish one eve, the mad ruler conceived an idea that he knew couldn't fail.

He sent one thousand men all across Lureland, "Find the lightest wood, sturdiest sails,

"And then build me a boat," he laughed hard as he spoke, and stared out to the Tearterran dunes.

The two lovers sat there completely unaware that their solace would be ending soon.

My daughter loves a poor Tearterran.
Shame.
I praise the gods her womb is barren.
Shame.
Lurelish blood should wed to diamonds
And not the dirt that's on that island.
Shame.
Even his name, how I despise it.
Shame.
He shames the throne on which Kitai sits.
Shame.
My Kiralay, I can't control her.
Our wants remain completely polar.
Our laws won't let me slit his throat.
I'll challenge him to build a boat.
Shame.

With a messaging bird, the mad king sent the word to the quaint island home that they kept.

When the message arrived, the would-be bride could have died on the very same spot where she wept,

But her lover was proud, vowing never to bow to the tyrannical king Kitai.

Angry, yet unafraid, he embraced Kiralay and went down to the beach for supplies.

Upon reaching the sands he could not understand how he could be expected to win,

But he carved out a boat, even got it to float, though it moved like a fish without fins.

Then he fashioned two oars, pulled his boat onto shore and sat down to consider a sail,

But the more that he thought, the more sadness it brought, for he knew he was certain to fail.

In the tide he lay down hoping only to drown and no longer be washed in his grief,

But the undertow stopped right before he could drop. He just floated on top like a leaf.

High above him the moon glowed the eeriest blue, two shades darker than any should be.

From below him approached the most wondrous of boats, ridden on by the god of the sea.

To the surface it bobbed, spewing forth such a fog that for moments all vision was ceased,

Then the fog disappeared, and the evening cleared with a wind that blew in from the East.

Next, the god of the sea, who was mad as could be, bellowed forth such a frightening voice

That he covered his ears, and he tried not to hear, though the boat builder hadn't a choice.

These waters here are sacred.
The magic here is real.
These waves are here to heal.
How dare you spoil its graces.
You don't deserve these waters.
Get back upon your island.
You're filthying my sea.
You have disgusted me.
My displeasure is rising.
You don't deserve these waters.

His head rang and it hurt, on his knees in the surf he fell, wailing and holding his ears.

Soon the tide came in reach and tossed him to the beach, adding insult to injuring tears.

Since he pitied the man, the sea god let him stand and then listened for what he would say.

The man felt rather weak, wasn't sure he could speak, but he rose to his feet, and he prayed.

I cannot win her hand
Unless you help me to.
I stand here on the sands
Petitioning to you.

Unless you help me to,
I'll never win this race.
Petitioning to you,
I'll never fall from grace.

I'll never win this race
Without your help to float.
I'll never fall from grace
With you beneath my boat.

Without your help to float,
I'll slowly sink away.
With you beneath my boat,
There is no need to pray.

I'll slowly sink away.
I stand here on the sands.
There is no need to pray.
I cannot win her hand.

Having heard the man's cries, the sea god closed his eyes, thinking hard about what had been said.

Then he reached onto shore, brushed away both the oars, and plucked up the man's boat from its bed.

In the waves with a splash, the sea god, with a laugh, dunked the boat as if washing it clean.

The god's eyes remained closed (the man left his exposed) while the vessel was sunken, unseen.

With a whoosh and a pop, the boat rushed to the top, spraying water high into the air.

Though it looked just the same as before, it had changed. Its new magic could not be compared.

To the craft the man ran, stumbling twice in the sand before falling face-first in the foam.

With a smile on his lips, the god lifted the ship and the man up, returning them home.

Then he turned to the sea, let the waves wander free and sailed closer to castle Kitai,

Where he laughed through his teeth before diving beneath with a grin and a wink of his eye.

With the morning sun high, Kiralay went outside where her lover still lay in his boat.

When she saw what he'd made, she tried hard to be brave, but felt certain his craft wouldn't float.

"With the race set for noon, we are certainly doomed," she said, turning and walking inside,

But her husband just smiled for he knew all the while that he would not be losing his bride.

Two new oars he then found by his boat on the ground, in the grass, where they'd been through the night.

And, along with these oars, dragged his boat down to shore, taking note that it felt rather light.

At the race he arrived feeling more than alive, though his craft looked as if it were dead.

There a man with a ship asked the boat builder if he would like to use driftwood instead.

And a crowd had amassed, and they all had their laughs at the young would-be husband's expense.

He just shrugged them aside, tossed his boat on the tide and waited for the race to commence.

Three times 'round the isle and back.
The marker was an island shack
That hurricanes had not yet toppled.
Perfect place to start and finish.
Royalty and poor alike
Came hither solely for the fight
That played between the gathered classes.
Which one would be first to finish?

On a wind from the west came Kitai with the best-looking vessel in all of the land.

The mast reached for the clouds, there was gold in the bow and the sails were the color of sand.

At the very tip-top of the mast waved the flag of Lureland made for Kitai.

On a midnight black field laid Kitai's golden seal striped with red for all those who have died.

Glancing over the side of his boat the man spied a blue flag and he started to smile.

On its face was a mass greener than any grass in the shape of the Tearterran isle.

He waved it from a nail in his mast where his sail was supposed to have captured the wind

Then he thrice crossed his heart, rowed his boat to the start and yelled out, "I'm ready to begin!".

It was then that the clouds, who 'til then, like the crowd, had been slowly increasing in sum

Suddenly multiplied and increased in their size, nearly blocking all light from the sun.

Then they shadowed the sea causing many to flee from their fear of the wrath of the gods.

And those who had no faith stayed right there in their places, just thinking the spectacle odd.

And among those who stayed while the world 'round them grayed and the race for the princess began

Was Syrena sans sea, just as dry as could be and disguised as a shell in the sand.

And she smiled to herself knowing what no one else could have known as the ships raced away:

That her father was there as a mist in the air and was holding the king's ship at bay.

The sun clichéd his way through the clouds
And they parted for him and then parted ways.
This seemed to wash the weight from my doubts.
I had done it at last, I'd won Kiralay.

Kitai returned to Lurelish soil
With his crown in his hand and head hanging low.
The ocean churned and started to boil
The sea god was appeased and laughing below.

My boat had weighed no more than a soul.
While I'd floated on waves, I'd floated on air.
I prayed the truth would never be told.
To speak more of this day, I never would dare.

On shore my boat still seemed rather light
So, I carried it home and hid it away.
By chance I roamed back into the night
Where the waves kiss the sand, I found Kiralay.

Her eyes were joyous, brimming with glee
And she blinked, letting loose a shower of pride.
She wiped her eyes and beckoned to me.
Chasing guilt from my heart, I sat by her side.

We spoke of marriage under the moon.
There on Tearterran sands we vowed we would wed.
Beside the tides, concealed by the dunes,
We embraced as the star shone bright over head.

With his wife by his side, he decided to hide from the truth and the ocean as well.

And he managed his time like he managed his mind: with his joy and his pain parallel.

After three years alone in their quaint island home, Kiralay sensed a seed in her womb,

So she prayed to the Earth leading up to the birth and thereafter she prayed to the moon.

Three more years rolled away and inside Kiralay grew another new island-bound soul

While the guilt that inside of her husband resided came closer to taking its toll.

While the guilt bit his brain, three more years passed again and he felt that the truth must be told,

For his secret was sharp, spoke to him in the dark, it was one he could no longer hold.

He informed Kiralay of the deity's aid, how his love for her drove him to lie.

With the children she strode to the ocean and rode to Kitai without saying goodbye.

With her daughters in tow, she let King Kitai know that her husband had brought them to shame

And the king, with a smile, called the man from the isle and forbade all from speaking his name.

Then, to make matters worse, and to make the man hurt, Kitai punished the man for his deeds.

That same vessel that won in the race they had run was the vessel in which he would leave.

"Also," added the king, "don't come back lest you bring me a treasure worth my Kiralay."

"No such treasure exists," cried the man with his fist clenched to hit all who stood in his way.

Just as he turned to leave his two ears did perceive two small voices in unison cry,

"Daddy, please hurry home," and he felt less alone, he would find such a treasure or die.

And with that thought he turned to the love he'd not earned, making bare his heart once more to speak.

Kiralay brought her ear closer to him to hear, for his voice had become rather weak.

I could race again, but it wouldn't really matter, Kiralay.
And I could just pretend that I never put the name Kitai to shame.
But lies are just a way to get your head around the things you know are true.
So does it matter, 'Lay, that I had to lie to prove my love to you?

I could race again, just a little thought I grapple with each day.
And I could just pretend that my life was always meant to be this way.
But lies are just good ways to get away just a little way.
So does it matter, 'Lay, that I don't want to be here anyway?

I should getaway...

I wonder who I'd be if you weren't such a part of who I am.
I'll always love the sea, but would I still love lying in the sand?

I couldn't find a way to win the race, and I never would, you know it's true.

So does it matter, 'Lay, that I had to lie to prove my love to you?

Why even pretend? We both know I would have never won your hand.
I should have told you long ago, but I didn't think you'd understand.
And lies are such good ways to get away just a little way.
If I were meant to stay, then I wouldn't still be here anyway.

You should getaway...

I'm afraid of fear, I'm afraid that fearing death will bring it near.
The truth I hid for years because I know too well the sound of falling tears.
But now I'll sail away from all that I hold dear and all that we've been through.
So does it matter, 'Lay that I had to lie to prove my love to you?

I haven't let you go, but I haven't held you near enough to show
The love I couldn't prove, now I'm lost because I couldn't grow
So where was my good way to get away just a little way?
The sky is turning gray; I should maybe leave before any rain.

Time to getaway...

His voice broken, he sulked from the palace, the bulk of his sadness marauding his soul.

At the base of the steps of the palace he wept, feeling separate, half of a whole.

There above him, the rains seemed to mimic his pain, dripping over the Lurelish town,

Washing houses in grief, rinsing dirt from the streets, as if racing his low spirits down.

I'm standing in the rain.
The crashing of every droplet
Echoes through my tempered skull
Like a deserted life
In which is thrown
A single, lonely heart.
The resounding raindrops cover me
And glide with gravity towards the street
As I,
And I alone,
Stand in the desert grief
And weep.
My soaking robes of city scene
Bring no oasis to my desolation.
The raindrops tame on paneless windows
Through which the eyes are watching me,
And in their apathy
They see
No courser world than misery.

As he turned to his home to prepare for his roaming, he felt a short tug on his sleeve.

An old lady stood there with the rain in her hair, unprepared to allow him to leave.

It is there, I know it is, for men have washed ashore
With tales of near escapes, with the fear of the god of the sea.
It is there, the treasure is, the Treasure of the Sea.
Worth a death to try and take.
But beware; I tell you this, the ocean god is wise.
His mood controls the winds, your true course you must not let him see.
It is true, not just a myth, the Treasure of the Sea.
The time is now, the quest begins.

To return to the life that he'd kept with his wife and his daughters he'd willingly die.

To Tearterra he rode, to his humble abode, and collected his boat and supplies.

He put many things in a large sack made of skins, which he tied to the nail on his mast,

And he took down the flag, stuffed it into his bag, and tried hard to let go of the past.

But, deep down in his heart, he felt certain his parting from home was to be evermore.

With his vessel in tow, he was ready to go, and wept all the way down to the shore.

So I bade farewell to my Tearterra,
Never to return again,
Nothing upon return to gain,
And set out towards the sun by sea.
T'was an island dwell, my sweet Tearterra.
Delta in the sea of time,

Farthest away from mainland eyes,
A perfect paradise just for me.
And my longings trailed behind my vessel,
Settled on the wake it made,
Forcing my soul to wake and wade
This one last time in well-known waters.
These same waters parted for my vessel,
Offering a ride my way,
Almost as if to guide my way
From all I love, my wife, my daughters.
In my sail there flowed a band of zephyrs,
Spinning me to find my path,
Almost as if to tip my craft
And see if my worthiness were sound.
Until finally a westward zephyr
Carried me towards the sun,
Shaking my boat 'til it was done,
And left me beyond the sight of ground.

Growing dry in the heat of the sun rays that beat down upon him through cool ocean air,

He discovered he'd not given all that much thought to the whens, and the whys and the wheres.

Funny how I had ambition
And watched it all just fade away.
Funny happiness came to me.
Funny how it wouldn't stay.

Funny how we have beginnings

Only to make it to the end.
Funny sadness has me crying
When tears of joy were Heaven-sent.

It's times like these that make me wonder
If life alone is worth the pain.
In times that follow you with desperation
You wonder what there is to gain.

If I could walk
Through the shadows of the forests,
If I could walk
Along the shores of quiet seas,
Would this void that I am lost inside
Finally let go of me?

Crazy how I wished for nothing
And felt surprised when nothing came.
Crazy times lead you to laughter
Crazy laughs are all the same.

Crazy how my life is changing
You search for truth, you lose your faith.
Crazy how I think I'm dying
It's a new beginning just the same.

It's times like these that make me wonder
Exactly why I feel such pain.
Inside my head I hear a consultation
And wonder if I'll go insane.

If I could walk
Through the shadows of the forests,
If I could walk
Along the shores of quiet seas,
Would this void that I am lost inside
Finally let go of me?

At the same exact time these thoughts ran through his mind, Kiralay suddenly felt alone.

On a parchment she wrote to her husband a note with the hopes that it may bring him home.

In a bottle she sealed up the note and her feelings and tossed them all into the waves.

One half of her felt he would die by himself, the other hoped he would be brave.

After all the memories have ceased to shimmer,
After all the sad goodbyes have lost their care,
After all the empty days become the normal,
I will leave, for after all, you won't be there.

I've been thinking of those days when we had laughter.
On some nights I even think about your smile.
But when I continue thinking there and after,
I keep thinking you've been gone for quite a while.

Rain's cliché, but there are circumstances hidden
Deep within your 'need to run away' façade.

So, my rain keeps falling as my heart stops living.
I look for sun, for you were there, and now you're gone.

Louder dreams have never entered my deep slumber
Than the dreams I have at night about your kiss.
Softest dreams, just like the quilt that I lie under.
Still, I wake up, and in this world you still are missed.

Happy days are saved for days when tears are seldom.
Unsung joy and fevered bliss I never see.
Every day I know the melancholy will come,
Because through all these lonely days you aren't with me.

After all the memories have ceased to shimmer,
After all the sad goodbyes have lost their care,
After all the empty days become the normal,
I will leave, for after all, you won't be there.

Out at sea the outcast, moving five times as fast as a boat without sails ought to move,

All at once lost his light as the day snapped to night and a cloud blued the glow of the moon.

Up, the waters splashed high, nearly caused a capsize as they washed the oars out of his grasp.

While the man nearly died, he managed to survive, though his satchel was ripped from the mast.

A wind pushed from the north and the ocean spewed forth the enraged deity of the sea.

A thick fog followed close, caused the outcast to choke, and left only its silver to see.

Though the man cowered down, the loud, earsplitting sound of the sea god's tirade hurt his head,

So, his eyes tightly shut, the man had no choice but to hear all the words the god said.

Who dares to travel on my seas
Without a proper sacrifice?
Without first giving praise to me?
Who dares to travel on my seas?
Give me your name, I'll be appeased.
If not your life will be the price.
Who dares to travel on my seas?
Without a proper sacrifice?

The response that he gave only served to enrage the god further than ever before.

He was tossed from his craft and landed with a crash on the sand of a desert isle's shore.

When, in pieces, his craft washed ashore the man laughed at how mad the sea god had become.

Given all he had said was "I'd rather be dead than to say who I am, or am from."

But the laughter stopped dead when it entered his head that he hadn't a means to escape.

At the ocean he spat, growing more aware that indignation had been a mistake.

His composure he kept, knowing that if he wept he would waste far too much precious light,
For he needed to eat, build a fire for heat, and build shelter for sleeping at night.

Knowing well of the gods, the man felt it was obvious that he would die on that isle,
For the wrath of the gods is a cruel wrath at best, like the wrath of a peer-driven child.

For twelve years, all alone on his water-locked home, the man dreamt of his sweet Kiralay
And he dreamt of his sweet daughters there on the beaches of home, he would reach them some day.

A paper boat, a bathtub sea, a moon made out of a seagull's egg.
When I close my eyes, it's what I see; when I open them I'm standing here instead.
I know about how salt can dry out any man who drinks his water from the sea
But I'd rather die by saline suicide than to let the sun and sand envelope me.
Nothing ever changes, nothing ever changes, no.
Stuck out here at sea – afloat in a misery that forever grows.
Nothing ever changes, nothing ever changes, no.
Stuck in misery – no one will come and save me, no.

There is no love, not here for me, for no one is around except the waves.

And I hear them laugh, and I hear them sing when the full moon takes his bow before the day.

The horizon keeps turning red and dolphins splash about in melodic dance.

There's so much life and still I feel dead as I fall into the sea's hypnotic trance.

Nothing ever changes, nothing ever changes, no.

Stuck out here at sea – afloat in a misery that forever grows.

Nothing ever changes, nothing ever changes, no.

Stuck in misery – no one will come and save me, no.

I can feel the moon, I can see the stars, but I'll never reach the sky from where I am.

I could build a boat, but it won't go far, so I'd rather stay right here on solid land.

Now, how am I supposed to feel if nothing here is real except the sand?

The days go by, the only things, and I can't seem to catch them with these hands.

Nothing ever changes, nothing ever changes, no.

Stuck out here at sea – afloat in a misery that forever grows.

Nothing ever changes, nothing ever changes, no.

Stuck in misery – no one will come and save me, no.

Syrena of the sea, filled with much clemency, had been watching the man's dilemma

And decided to pay him a visit one day as a crab with a broken antenna,

And the castaway, being a passionate being, ate all but that crab from his trap.

He just set her aside, tossed her into the tide, and yelled out to her not to come back.

On the isle we ate what we could catch and nothing more than that.
We fished and dove, set and checked traps to bring our dinners home.
I am proud to say that never so cold was a Tearterran soul
As to eat a creature from the sea who wasn't fit to roam.
So go back to your damnation and let me return to mine
Unless you wish to witness me devouring your kind.

If, perchance, you see the sea god, tell him that I still am well.
I'll bide my time, escape this hell, and take his treasure, too.
And I'll make it home, back to Kiralay and my daughters, who wait
I'll achieve all this, I tell you, and there's nothing he can do.
Now go back to your damnation and let me return to mine.
You have no need for friendship when your enemy is time.

When three years had been spent, Syrena once more went to the island in brilliant disguise.

She appeared as an oyster, or rather, the pearl that was waiting, with patience, inside.

And while diving, the man, with a rock in his hand, cracked the oyster and pilfered the pearl

And he stood on the sands staring into his hand, feeling proud when his fingers uncurled.

Glistening, like his eye was his pretty new prize, how he yearned to give it to his wife,

And he yearned to be free, back at home and at peace and return to his Tearterran life.

It so hurt him to know that he couldn't yet hope to return to his sweet daughters' arms

For this treasure was small, wasn't worthy at all, in comparison, only a charm.

It is like the sea, it has no bounds, my love for Kiralay.
How did she ever come to love me?
She was born into the ruling class of Lureland
As Princess Kiralay the Lovely.
And when we were young, my Kiralay, she taught me how to laugh.
Her father threatened to take my tongue
Yet I still continued yelling out my love for her.
The gods themselves couldn't lull my lungs.
It is curious, a sweet taboo, my love for Kiralay.
The ruling class all wish to harm me.
All the mainland eyes that fall on me are murderous
A fact I seldom found alarming,
For Lurelish laws keep them at bay, forbidden are their wants.
They shun Tearterrans for we are poor.
What they do not understand is our happiness.
They have so much, still they yearn for more.

Thus, he tossed the pearl back, ever blind to the fact that Syrena had been in his grasp.

Though, he felt less alone, like a face had been shown of a friend he had known in his past.

Three more years passed again and the man felt such pain as to give in at last to defeat.

One last letter he wrote Kiralay on a note made from leaves he had found on the beach.

A gull feather had been what he'd used as a pen, and his ink was the sap of a tree,

And who watched all the while, with a sad, loving smile, but Syrena, Princess of the Sea.

That last letter was dark, for he'd given it parts of the heart he would no longer need

And the ink nearly smeared when it met with a tear that his eyes were too blurry to see.

I am boneless, weak and arid; be me bondless, free, released.
Could not find the love-worth treasure, be me finally deceased.
Mine own eyes are drained and sapless, dehydrated, vacant, raw.
Blame it on the path I traveled; blame it on the pain I saw.
Better yet, let blame be buried by the sands I lay beneath,
Right alongside all my worries, evermore is out of reach.
Tell our daughters daddy loves them, tell them not to wait for me.
Tell them while I searched for solace, I was swallowed by the sea.

Now I lay me down in water, sink me slowly 'til I sleep.
Years alone upon this island, now I'll have eternity.
Find a lover, someone worthy, wary he be not a knave.
Judge him not by what he's gotten, rather, judge by what he gave.
All is well in Purgatory, burden not your heart with grief.
Time, it eats away at glory; evermore is out of reach.

By the time this letter finds you, I will have lost misery.
Do not bother searching for me; I was swallowed by the sea.

This dark letter he wrapped in more leaves, and in sap, before casting towards where he'd been,
Then laid down in the tide, with his mouth opened wide, and attempted to sink yet again.

When the sea floor he met, he exhaled, giving death his permission to salvage his soul.
Syrena, with one eye on the man as he died, read the note and felt forced to condole.

With a voice like the sky that spread far, and reached wide, she sang out to her sea-dwelling friends.
In response to her song came a crab ten times longer and wider than all of its kin.

And this king of all crabs, how he had such a laugh when he saw the man sunk in the surf,
But Syrena was stern, and her face showed concern, so the king of all crabs went to work.

With three clicks of his claws, the king crab seemed to call out to all other crabs within reach
Who obeyed his command, crawled up out of the sand, and transported the man to the beach.

And they squeezed all the water from lungs like an orange with only the weight of their shells

Before crawling back down to their homes in the ground, ever certain the man would be well.

Then the king of all crabs bowed his claws to his master and dove to the sea's darkest depths.

Syrena, on the sands, had her lips to the man's and was breathing air into his chest.

And this air, as it were, belonged only to her, and her father, who'd given her life,

And her long-estranged brother, whose land-loving mother refused to be her father's wife.

It was this very air that allowed her to bear living under the sea as she did.

Though her father would yell, she just smiled, for she felt that the air had been her air to give.

As she started to cry one, then both of his eyes opened side by side, seeing her there,

So she kissed him once more before changing her form to a seagull's and took to the air.

The man shrugged as he stood, for he knew the sun could cause delusions to darken the mind,

But he could not ignore the boat docked at the shore that Syrena left for him to find.

And the questions invoked as he walked to the boat would have left most men withered and weak,

But a voice on the wind singing praises to him gave him courage, allowed him to speak.

I don't want to be afraid of what you could be
But I don't want things to stay the same.
We all have to change someday, if you believe in me
I'll make sure that a change will come your way.

A million seashells along the beach
But none of them seemed to speak to me.
With water in my eyes and water in my hands
I dug down deep.

A million seashells beneath my feet
But all of them seemed just out of reach.
Somehow, I found my sister in the sand
Down by the sea.

The tide will come in tonight as I sail from the shore
And I'll wonder if you're alright this time.
These waves reflect a light of a heart so torn
And I wonder which beach will find this sister of mine.

A million seashells along the beach
But none of them seemed to speak to me.
With water in my eyes and water in my hands
I dug down deep.

A million seashells beneath my feet
But all of them seemed just out of reach.

Somehow, I found my sister in the sand
Down by the sea.

I don't want to be afraid of where you might go
But I don't want you to stay in pain.
The sand of time will change someday, if you believe in me
I'll make sure that they change grain by grain.

I don't want to be afraid of who you might be
But I don't think you understand.
Only the waves could ever sing exactly what you mean to me
You are my sister in the sand.

As he'd once more survived watery suicide, he felt certain his fate had been sealed.

He would sail to the lair of the sea god, and there, steal the treasure or strike up a deal.

Knowing not where he was, he sailed westward, because it afforded the fastest escape

For this island had broken him, drained him of hope, and he'd had about all he could take.

As the sunset approached on his third day afloat, he was thankful for night's cooling dew.

He'd forgotten one thing, of all things not to bring; he'd forgotten fresh water to use.

And his throat had grown dry, and it hurt just to sigh, and the sun only forced him to sweat.

Though the cold bit his skin, and his body had thinned, in the night he could dream and forget.

I choose to dream to pass the time.
So far away from anything,
Upon this sea so punishing,
A punishment that fits my crime.

Into the sea I ought to climb,
Inside this vessel, suffering,
I choose to dream to pass the time,
So far away from anything.

For when awake I feel that I'm
Too near the death the sea can bring.
To life, in dreams, I tend to cling.
So, not awaiting Death's bells' chime,
I choose to dream to pass the time.

When the sun rose again, he forgot where he'd been, if only for a moment of peace.

When that moment had passed, he remembered too fast, and was taken aback with defeat.

He survived through the days, 'til the sun went away just by laying as still as could be.

And the moon brought to him that refreshing, cool wind he had come to know fondly as Free.

Break midnight's calm, caress my skin,

My Free, my loving wind.
Ice for my lungs and soul within,
My Free, my loving friend.
You give me peace, you give me sleep,
You help me to survive.
You help me with remembering
Why I must stay alive.
I give nothing, you ask for less
I still desire more.
You comfort me from East and West,
Console from South and North.
I cannot move, you can't be curbed,
My Free, my loving wind.
One more companion undeserved.
My Free, my loving friend.

When the day passed again, he expected his friend to come visit him during the night.

When he started to miss his companion's cool kiss, he woke startled, surrounded by lights.

And these magical lights, they glowed almost as bright as the sun on a clear summer day.

And who saw them likewise with two fear-swollen eyes, but the pensive Princess Kiralay.

I am ignoring the lights on the water.
They remind me of funeral fires and the sea god's eyes,
Of my husband the liar, that my love may have died.
I am ignoring those lights there dancing on the water

And reflected in my tears as I cry.
I am ignoring my sense of foreboding.
I can only hope Lureland's shores will be safe from harm,
That those lights are a beacon and not just an alarm.
I am ignoring my sense of frightening foreboding
And the lights by which I will not be charmed.

Fearing magic, the king had his guardians bring her and both of her daughters at once
To a tower room high up in Castle Kitai where he stationed a sentry in front.

And the sentry who watched at the very tip-top of the tower, outside of the room
Felt his fate fluctuate like he'd cleared from his slate a once-written prerequisite doom.

At that moment, at sea, the man, sans his friend Free, felt much braver than ever before.
He was ready to die for a chance at what lie on the sea's subterranean floor.

The lights flashed on the water, rather, shone and went away
Providing me with temporary vision, I could see
That I was headed nowhere, rather, nowhere beckoned me.
The answers had to be here lest my searching be in vain.
I yelled my daughters' names aloud and dove into the sea.

The night had been disorder, rather, order left with Free
And all I had remaining was my will to stay alive.

My fear had long-since vanished, rather, vanishing was I
Into the dark abyss to where I'd find my destiny.
I dove down deeper still, and felt my sobered spirits rise.

My mind ignored the pressure, rather, pushed the pain aside.
I realized that I'd abandoned any need for air.
I pushed into the darkness, rather, darkness drew me there
With no care whatsoever whether I would stay alive.
The deeper I was drawn, the deeper felt was my despair.

Yet soon I found the treasure, rather, found the sea god's lair.
I felt no warmth inside, a cold had settled in my chest,
And still my heart was hopeful, rather, hope still lingered best.
I swam into the chasm with the sea god unaware
And surfaced in a lake of sorts peacefully drawing breath.

Breathing air yet again made him feel alien to the life he had lived on the land

But he hadn't the time to consider his find, nor determine a workable plan

For the lake's surface showed he did not swim alone, he'd been joined by the fin of a shark

Of the dangerous type, yes, the great, angry white had arrested the man in its arc.

Apprehension ensued and his disquietude caused the man to call out for support

And the shark, at the sound, turned completely around, dove below, and abandoned the port.

To the edge, just as fast as he could, the man splashed, secrecy no longer
a concern

And he dragged himself clear of the lake and his fears drawing closer
to danger, in turn.

Though to enter the lake had not been a mistake, to exit it most
certainly had,

For this danger had killed men of far stronger will and had driven the
weaker willed mad.

Shuddering, looking back, he considered the facts and soon walked to
the edge for a look.

Leaning in to inspect, the man saw his reflection – the bait, and bit
into the hook.

Self, I see myself
Here, where I need help.
On the water's face.
Clear, I face myself.

There, it moves away,
Mirror set adrift.
Did not stir the lake
Does this thing exist?

Center of the glass.
Still, it mimics me.
Echo of my mind,
Speculum released.

Once was paper-flat
Now it takes a shape.
Same form as my own,
Eyes and mouths agape.

Shape must give us weight,
For this specter here
Sinks into the lake,
Halfway disappears.

Gasping out for air,
Churning water now.
Cannot help but stare,
Watch this specter drown.

Yet is this not me?
Should I not give aid?
Were he truly me,
Should he not be saved?

As he sinks below,
Leaping is my heart.
In my panicked state
Flames of knowledge spark.

Self, I am myself.
That is something else.
Lest it learns to swim
It cannot be helped.

With one last look of fear, the specter disappeared, sinking quickly down into the dark

Leaving no sign of life, though the man swore he'd spied, sinking also, the tail of a shark.

"More tricks meant to alarm, they can cause me no harm just as long as I keep to my goal,"

The man said, standing tall, and examined the walls, searching hard for traversable holes.

When he found one his size, just as high, just as wide, he pushed through it wide-eyed and alert.

On the tips of his toes, breathing in through his nose, further into the lair he lurked.

Soon he came to a hall with amazing, high walls made of coral and blue-colored glass.

Large and dark shadows crawled just behind the blue walls in the shapes of the beasts that swam past.

Full of hope, through the room the man scampered, presuming that soon he'd find that which he sought

But the room would not end, and the shadows tormented him. Mentally he was distraught.

Turning back not an option, he looked to the top of the wall he had come to know well

And he noticed a beam of light just at the ceiling. This wall was the door to his cell.

He walked up to the center and pushed it to enter, not budging the giant doors much.

"Not the first fence I've found," he said, looking around for a lever or button to touch.

He noticed that the wall moved the more that he talked, "Sliding slowly, but sliding at least,"

So he filled his lungs up almost more than enough and blew until the lock was released.

He exhaled not a word as the shadows converged at the point where his breath had been blown

And the wall opened wide, revealing there inside the sea god, fast asleep on his throne.

The mere size of the god in his eyes left him shocked, he felt smaller than ever before

But the god shrank in size, rose, and opened his eyes, and then softly he said, "Close the door."

Knowing not what to do, the man turned, and he blew, for his breath was what widened the wall,

But the god had not spoken to he who had opened the door, nor had seen him at all

For, just to the right of him, almost in hiding, was she who had kept him in life.

She was just a faint glow, if a sound, would be low, like a humming-bird's flapping in flight.

With a wink and a grin, she created a wind with the tips of the fingers alone

Which then slid the wall back into place with a crack in the place where the man's clue had shone.

With his task back in mind, the man scampered to find any sign of the treasure about.

Yet, the god, unamused, yelled, "Contemptible fools! Don't you think I have figured you out?"

He spat foam as he screamed, shook the spine of Syrena, and froze the man's feet where he stood.

"As blind as I may be, I am able to see when my daughter is up to no good!

"And this fool you have brought to the Palace of Dark Depths, he reeks of the air and the land

"And he comes here intending to steal what most men have all seen but do not understand

"But you both are mistaken, the facts of our fate are not separate, rather, are one

"For no man could have kept the Blue Breath in his chest, nor dove down to the depths he has come."

"Father, what do you mean?" "Leave us now, sweet Syrena, for we two have much to discuss."

Though it brought her dismay, Syrena did obey, leaving fast, without much of a fuss.

"Look deep into your soul, Aridamissa.
For there lies dormant
Proof of life
Beyond what you have known."

"What is this name you say? Aridamissa?"

"It is the name
We give to those
Who've lived away from home.
In truth, you are my son, Aridamissa.
The name you use is
Proof of that
A fact you've always known."

"I won't believe your lies! You're not my father!"

"It is the name
I gave to he
Whose bloodline is my own."

"Just give me what I came for, keep your stories.
Forgive me if I
Fail to fall
For yet another sleight."

"In fact, what you have come for is your story."

"The treasure, now!

Or there won't be
A change of tides tonight.
Make haste, you fiend, at once, forget your stories.
Don't think that I would
Fail to fight.
My care for you is slight."

"The treasure is your home, it is Tearterra."

"The treasure, no,
It can't be true
These words, they can't be right."

"Look deep into your soul, son of Tearterra,
For you are truly
King of all
The land that touches sea."

"Yet we live weak, and thin, sons of Tearterra."

"You live upon
An island made
For you, how can this be?
I made one paradise, son, one Tearterra.
And you were to be
King upon
The Treasure of the Sea."

"Kitai, he lives upon Tearterran tears now.
We live upon,

I do suppose,
The fact that we are free."

"That treacherous Kitai, I'll drown his cities!"

"You cannot do that!"

"Yes, I can!"

"My family is there!"

"Then you must hurry now and bring them hither."

"What of the rest?"

"They'll learn to swim."

"That fate is hardly fair."

The sea god was enraged, and his choice had been made, so debating would waste precious time.

Though the man knew this well, he still let out a yell of defeat in the depths of his mind.

To the blue, shadowed, doors he ran, blowing, of course, for Syrena had locked them again.

As they opened, he saw Syrena in the hall, smiling widely, "Prepare to ascend."

She had stood, for a while, in the hall, with that smile, listening to the parley inside,

Then away she had slipped to prepare him a ship, coming back just in time to be spied.

"My blind heart always knew." "So, my aide, it was you. I remember your voice from the waves.

And the old lady's song, it was yours all along, and the kiss," "There is no time to waste.

"You must hurry at once, for the full moon has come, and the wrath of a god never waits,

On the surface a ship is in waiting. The kiss was a dream. Go and save Kiralay."

To the lake he ran, and, to the surface he swam and sailed off with more speed than the wind,

Which left, somewhat confused, Syrena, by the blue, shadowed wall pondering her new kin.

From syrup seas, on mighty wind,
I sailed for home, with fear within
To warn my wife, and kids, and kin
The tidal storms would soon begin.
The moon hung high to lead me home.
The stars – my charts, oh, how they shone.
The waves beneath were tipped with foam.
A calmer night I'd never known.
I knew what just behind me loomed:
The worst presage one could presume.

The sea god's anger all too soon
Would treacherously tell their doom.
The lights still shone on water's face.
A flag above me had been placed.
The same flag found before the race.
It somewhat symbolized my haste.
The treasure I had found inside
Of my desire for my bride,
For that same love had never died.
This treasure could not be denied.
I sailed for home, where I belong
Surrounded by Syrena's song
And one fact lingering too long:
Should have been ruler all along.

When the shore came in sight, the man's heart beat with might and his eyes released buckets of joy.

And his mind overflowed with sweet thoughts of old, tattered love, and his time as a boy.

At the Tearterran beach, the storm just out of reach, he docked not just his ship, but his pride.

Over shoulder he glanced, hoping there was a chance he could save all he loved from the tide.

Under feet now, the sands, helped to balance the man, who'd grown used to the sway of the sea

And the balance of time served to dizzy his mind – he remembered home differently.

Dead seaweed, dry and brown, covered most of the ground with a surface of sinewy strings.

"Quite ironic," he thought, "I left paradise poor and I come home to hell as a king."

Upon reaching the mouth of the dune-path his doubts crowded him like the overgrown weeds.

Though he'd come very far, he'd been gone very long, and on confidence guilt tends to feed.

Not a moment to spare, smelling salt on the air, the man ran up the path to his house

Where he found that the vines had grown long over time and his dwelling had long been without

Any semblance of care, for a moment he stared and thought hard about time and its ways.

How it could not be tamed, how it could not be bought, how it kept him from his Kiralay.

"Tell me that you're well,"
I imagined she'd say,
Though I knocked and walked away.
It was just as well,
For no answer came.
Not a parting of windowshades.
Spent my youth with her
Now my hair has grown gray,
So I rapped and walked away.
I could not return

To her heart again
I had lost my dear Kiralay.
While my daughters aged
I'd been lost on the sea
So I doubt they'll know it's me.
Which is just as well,
For I've caused them grief.
More than even my eyes have seen.
Spent their youth without
Any notion of peace
And the doubts they had of me
And my swift return,
And their hearts' caprice.
Such sadness is never serene.

Weighed with woe, the man wept, as the gulls quit their nests and the turtles fled into the sea.

Slow, the sea came and crept over all that was left and submerged the man up to his knees.

As his ship drifted near his eyes cleared out their tears and all sound suddenly disappeared.

In his vessel he climbed, checked the sun for the time, and noticed a new sound in his ears.

Like a whistle, but low, and the sound seemed to grow ever closer, and louder, in turn.

When its origin cleared the horizon, the fear in the man was replaced by concern.

He no longer feared death, for the air in his chest, and these waters would keep him alive.

He was worried that soon his home would be consumed by the wave growing before his eyes.

And the wave did, indeed come down hard, with such speed that the man hadn't time to lament.

Thus, with one heavy breath, he surveyed what was left, what was gone, and what had been exempt.

Over yonder he spied something fixed on the tide, just as still as the sun in the sky.

Sailing closer, he spat when he realized that it was part of the castle Kitai,

But a voice coming from that which sat like the sun and had lasted the wrath of the sea

Was a voice he knew well, for he'd traveled to Hell and come back just to hear its decree.

There, through window of stone, being wet by the foam from the tips of the waves splashing by

Were his love and his life, his daughters and his wife, safe from harm. They had somehow survived.

And the sentry was there, for he too had been spared by the self-serving act of Kitai

Who had drowned with the rest and was now at the depths of the ocean, his crown by his side.

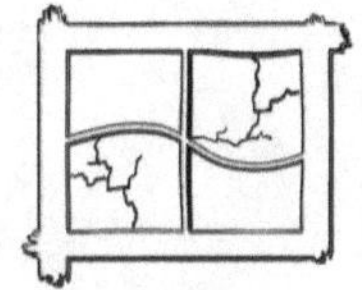

THE CROSSING

Staunch the bleeding.
That won't heal, there is no time.
Must keep moving.
Can't stay here, not far behind.
I can hear them
Headed for the timberline.
If you follow
You'll be difficult to find.

Dogs grow tired,
Men get lost and trails go cold.
Keep your money.
You can burn it when we're cold.
Tiny fires,
Nothing large enough for smoke.
Daytime only.
After dawn has fully broken.

See those mountains?
Once we cross between the peaks,

They won't follow.
You'll have freedom, so to speak.
Match my pace now.
We have rendezvous to keep.
Stay awake now,
Or be left right where you sleep.

Lunar lantern
See it hanging in the sky?
Always guiding.
Lighting paths where danger lies.
Mother told me
It's the Great Coyote's eye.
Always watching.
Gave her peace when she was dying.

Leave that water.
It's not clean enough to drink.
Eat what I eat
Or die sooner than you think.
Almost there now.
Must feel like you're on the brink
Of collapsing
Eyes feel heavy when you blink?

Check your bandage
Get infected, lose your hand.
We'll keep going
Just so long as you can stand.
Off the trail now.

Through the valley just as planned.
Won't be followed.
Won't be safe, though, understand me?

Not forever,
But, yes, this does take a while.
Grown accustomed.
Started when I was a child.
Ninety crossings.
Memorized each single mile.
Always danger.
Here the paths themselves are wild.

Step where I step
There are traps here set by men
Long before now.
We were fearful people then.
Wiser now, though.
Know that all things have an end.
Time is precious.
Better ways for us to spend it.

Almost there now.
Focus on the steps ahead.
When we get there
We'll have water, rest, and bread.
You're a strong one.
Could have stayed back there instead.
None would blame you.
Most who tried to cross are dead.

I have seen them.

Fallen, all along the trail.

Hope is fragile.

Often, hunger will prevail.

Some die walking,

Marching on to no avail.

Eyes wide open,

Ever focused on their failings.

Best keep close now.

This is where The Crossing starts.

All your close calls,

I would call the easy part.

You'll be tested.

Keep your reasons close at heart.

Listen closely.

There's more knowledge to impart:

Bundle up now.

Keep on moving once we're in.

Never falter.

What you feel won't be the wind.

That's The Crossing

That you feel against your skin.

Frozen fury.

Colder than a thousand winters.

Ninety crossings.

Never lost a single soul.

Ninety-one soon,
Once we make it to the goal.
Faster, faster,
Lest The Crossing take its toll.
One direction.
Like you're falling through a hole.

On your feet now.
Dying here would be a waste.
Look, you made it.
Hardest thing you've ever faced?
Let's get moving.
Use that new will you've embraced.
Make up time now.
Catch the setting sun we're chasing.

Check your bandage.
I have one left, if you need.
Hand still working?
Good, it's best if we proceed.
Hours left now.
Could be less with any speed.
Push yourself now.
Worth the pain once we succeed.

Tiny houses
Used to dot these mountainsides.
Lights through windows,
Warm and glowing hearths inside.
War came through here.

Left them nowhere to reside.
They adapted.
Now The Crossing is providing.

Gives us shelter
From that place you've always known.
I was born there.
My first crossing was my own.
I was small then.
Mother taught the dos and don'ts.
Forty crossings.
When she died, I crossed alone.

Ninety crossings.
Always with someone in tow.
Never backwards.
People come; they never go.
Like a river.
No one fights against the flow.
Should you wish to,
Know The Crossing's ever blowing.

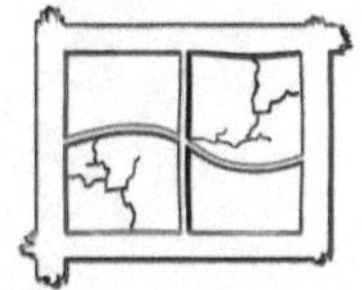

THE STOCKPILE INITIATIVE

We needed ammunition constantly.
On the battlefield we did not covet food and sleep,
We prayed for ammunition.

We started The Stockpile Initiative.
From the carcasses we took whatever guns were left.
Unanimous decision.

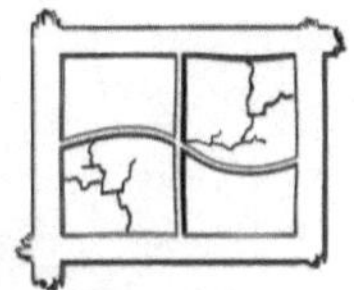

WELTERWEIGHT

The trees

Are not supposed to dance

Into

The wind.

I have seen them sway.

I have seen them duck like boxers.

Rope-a-dope.

These trees fight

A different fight.

The wind can not be beaten.

Still, they lean.

They lean into the wind.

When the wind is a breeze

They stand tall.

They reach like grass for the sun.

When the wind is a gust.

They push back.

I would not cut them if I were you,

Nor tap them for their sap.

I would not threaten them with fire.

Or trust them not to move when no one is watching.

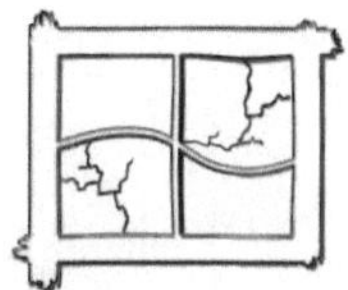

BROTHER! FROM AUTOMATE!

"Remember, you're only a Brother," they said.
I only heard once, though it stayed in my head.
I, great pretender, ignored their request
And left for the city instead.

I purchased a ticket for seven-oh-nine.
"The big city stop's at the end of the line!"

The train engineer would not let me aboard.
"A man made of steel's an affront to the lord.
Soul. You ain't got one. Them's gears in your chest.
That there's where a soul should be stored."

The train engineer tore my ticket in two.
"You're only a Brother, so what can you do?"

With no other options, I followed the tracks,
The city ahead and the sun on my back.
Lost, with direction, en route to the world,
With only my traveling sack.

"When you see a Brother, you know right away!
Their eyes are aglow and they're AutoMate gray!"

A mile from the city, it started to rain.
I hid in a barn with an old aeroplane.
Rust, dust, and hay bales all welcomed me in
With nary a hint of disdain.

No one gave me feelings. I feel that was wrong.
Perhaps I have felt certain things all along.

The storm sauntered on, dragging with it the clouds.
I walked through a field that had long gone unplowed.
Mud, freshly minted, marked proof of my wake,
A sign said, *'No Brothers Allowed'*.

"A Brother robot can pick produce all day
Then bundle the product and haul it away!"

A scarecrow was watching me, birds on its arms,
It's hay decomposing like most of the farm.
Crows cackled madly and took to the sky
Afraid I may wish them some harm.

I undressed the scarecrow and put on its clothes.
The first set of clothing that I ever chose.

With mud-covered clothing and hat on my head
I walked to the road, set to go where it led.

Al, passing trucker, said, "You city bound?
Jump into my truck bed instead!"

My mud-covered hands made a sort of disguise,
Just like the big hat pulled low over my eyes.

Night fell on the city just as we arrived.
Al found some free parking on Avenue Five.
Lights, sound, and motion surrounded the truck.
Never had I felt so... *alive.*

The buildings stretched on further than could be seen
With more sounds and lights pushed around in between.

Al said his goodbyes and we went to shake hands
"You're only a Brother. Thought you were a man."
Shocked, somewhat angered, he shoved me aside.
"If I were in charge you'd be banned."

I walked through the city to take in the views
Then sat on a bench, near a bank, unamused.

This was not the city I'd dreamed of before.
Most Brothers were servants, berated, ignored.
Some, who were rusted, stood waiting in vain
For owners who want them no more.

"The AutoMate warranty covers all parts,
Including replacement if Brother won't start!"

A Brother fell over and laid on the ground.
The people walked over instead of around.
Sad, I tried helping. A woman stepped in.
Said, "You must be from out of town."

"Just leave it. It's only a Brother, you see?
Collectors will come. You can just leave it be."

I aided the Brother. It offered me thanks.
The woman just laughed. "What a wonderful prank!"
"No," I tried saying. My voice was drowned out.
Alarms rang from inside the bank.

"You're Brother can't save you from physical harm,
But if you're in trouble, they'll sound the alarm!"

The woman was frightened and hurried away.
The Brother left too (no one told it to stay).
Shouts, screams, and gunshots mixed with the alarms.
The scene had become disarray.

A man who came running while loading a gun
Said "I call the bounty! Go call nine-one-one!"

I followed him in without making the call.
The phone booth said, *'No Brother Use'*, after all.
Death, blood and chaos all welcomed us in
With the bullet holes dotting the walls.

"A Brother can carry whatever you need!

Just tell it to pick up and then to proceed!"

A figure came carrying bags from the vault.
The bounty hunter cocked his guns and said, "Halt."
Kneeling, the figure slumped over and died
While saying, "It was not my fault."

The hunter of bounties said, "My name is Reece,"
Then fired shots at the recently deceased.

"It's okay, it's only a Brother," he said.
He laughed and he shot the robot in its head.
Gyros and fluid spilled onto the floor
With nary a tear to be shed.

"Though Brothers can't offer you blood, sweat, or tears,
They'll toil without trouble for multiple years!"

More bullets than Reese had intended took flight.
The robber, with murder and Reese in his sights,
Grabbed, while still shooting, both bags with one hand
And exited into the night.

Reese reached for his guns while his life slipped away.
"Why didn't you stop him?" He asked, with dismay.

"I'm sorry, I'm only a Brother," I said.
I knelt down and took the hat off of my head.
Stood, found an exit that went through the rear,
And left for the country instead.

"A Brother robot never has an intent.
They come when they're called and they go where they're sent!"

234

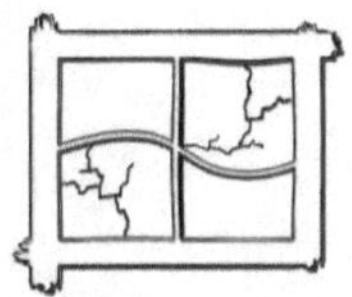

PALMISTRY

Darkness is an issue.
Crumbling walls, rough surface.
Glass-like protrusions
Threaten
The hand that guides me.
These walls -
They bite the hand, it feeds them.
These walls
Will lead me to a door.
These walls
Are a river.
I seek to find the sea.
This river
Is far too greedy.
This river
Drinks far too much of me.

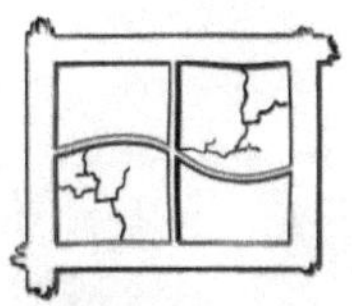

TEA

240

They pour the water.
The water starts to brown.
The water rises
In the cup.
They put the kettle down.

They lift the tea bag.
They wrap the string around
The bag.
They squeeze it.
Satisfied,
They set the tea bag down.

They pour the dairy.
It's white swirls with the brown
And, with the sugar,
Disappears.
They stir the tea around.

They lift the teacup.

Their fingers curl around
The mug.
Their fingers
Feel the warmth.
They make a sipping sound.

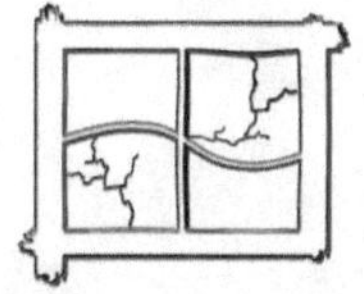

PENMANSHIP

Plots sewn in concentric circles
Readers reap in farmers rows
Writing is remembering
Reading is the long repose

I was penning spells of passion
Knowing they would not be read
Thought of love lost long ago
Something that she always said

Words these days are loose and shapeless
Hers were polished, cold and hard
Cut me deep like river flow
Bedrock of my heart left scarred

Placed my journal on the bookshelf
Memories are noisy ghosts
Found forgotten photo books
Ones that featured her the most

Voices carry over water
Twice as far when over time
Heard hers loudly in my ear
Still demanding, still sublime

Chasing sleep, drank deep of bourbon
Pictures chased me into dreams
Still, her voice rang on, unstopping,
Whispered through my pillow seams

When I woke, the smell of cooking
Chased regret and pain away
She was standing in the kitchen
'Told you I'd be back some day."

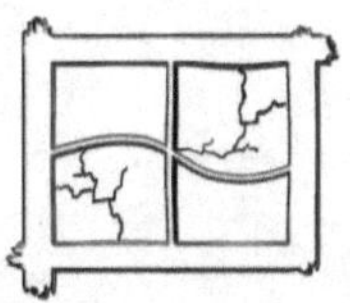

ESCAPE

The waters-turned-gas could not get in, and gravity released me.
The pod I escaped in stopped its spin; the ocean floor beneath me.
Outside of my shell I heard a sound: the sea around me heating.
A hull needs to cool, I need that too, panic is self-defeating.

I float like a yolk inside this egg. The pressure builds around it.
The pressure builds, too, inside my head. The metal creaks, I pound
it.
The radio dial just spins and spins. The static never changes.
No maydays today, it's just as well. I'm not sure what the range is.

The Cleaner will sweep away the parts remaining of my shuttle.
Just as he did with my past affairs: the other ships I've scuttled.
The radars will note a pod touched down; they'll think themselves
mistaken.
I find it odd this safety pod is a tomb of my own making.

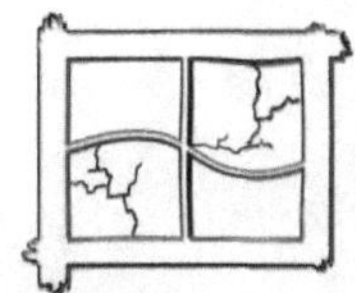

THE ROAD HOME

I ride upon an ebon steed, my speed not fast enough for me.
You stand – dead center of the road, thick dust licks at your feet.

"Whoa," I cry. My horse rears up. You show no signs of fear.
I dismount and call out to you.
You do not seem to hear.
You kiss my stallion's midnight side. It strides towards the glade.
I gaze into your crimson eyes as you whisper this: "Be brave."

A strike of lightning from the skies lifts up my horse and out I cry:
"How can I possibly go on if my companion were to die?

I realize now that to this glade I'm evermore a slave."
You kiss me gently, take my hand,
And whisper this: "Have faith."
Suddenly, as though reborn, my steed is now a mare
With pearl-white mane it beckons me: "Come to me if you dare."

I mount the mare, and as I do, my sword and armor are renewed.
As well, my head is filled with thoughts I'd lost, but also knew.

I study you for you seem to know the path I am to take.
I ask, "Should I be going now?"
You answer this: "Just wait."
As if to follow your command the skies bring forth the sun.
Before me now the road seems dead, behind me life has sprung.

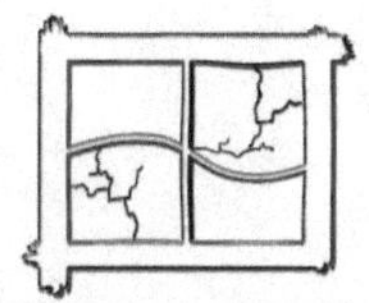

OLYMPUS

"How distasteful,
And, Man, we made sure
To keep life hard enough to keep y'all grateful
But y'all ain't thankful.
Don't even give thanks no more.
Thanksgiving's lost all meaning.
I hate y'all."
"But, God,"
"I ain't done
Of ours y'all ain't sons.
One of us said don't touch his fucking apples.
Y'all ate one.
We ought to just destroy the whole Earth that y'all made from.
End it all and start it all over from day one."
"There was no day one!
That lie's been made up!
I'm sick and tired of hearing it - it's time you faced up."
"Fessed up."
"Okay, just
Allow me to say what's

Been on my mind, I find that y'all don't hear when we pray much.
Or offer any help."
"Well, could it be you don't say much?"
"You call yourself a god?"
"You know what? Back in the day such
Blatant disrespect would get your life,
As you say, 'touched'.
You're nothing but dirt."
"Well, then, you're nothing but mud's crutch.
I'm sick of leaning on you gods.
How long since you've been just?"

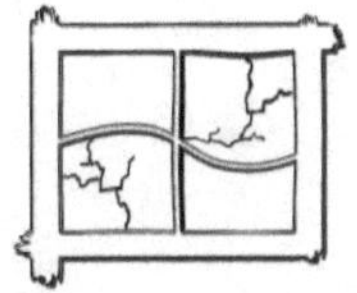

HEAVYWEIGHT

When you swing at me, you're slow,
Predictable.
Have you seen defeat?
It's all you'll ever know.
Must have anchor feet, no flow.
In situ, Bro?
Heavyweights like me will beat you
Just for show.
First time in my ring?
It's time you learned the ropes.
How's that canvas feel?
It's all you'll ever know.

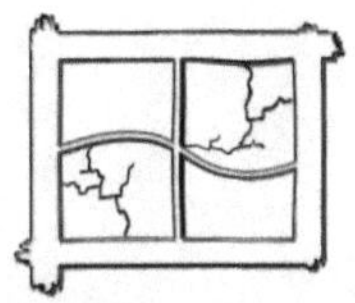

Peace

Men had come from the shore saying death was waiting for
Any person, rich or poor, who refused their maker's love.
They brought with them many gifts, told us gods and saints exist,
That if we didn't yield to this. Death would rain down from above.

Righteous anger's what they earned. We told them never to return,
If they did, then we would burn the pretty ships they sailed here on.
We had no need for wicked lies. The gaoler Peace controls the skies.
We assumed their departure nigh. We soon found out that we were
wrong.

In the night the clouds arrived. Made of smoke, they blinded eyes.
There was nowhere we could hide, There was no weapon we could
use.
From the shore a message came: should we praise their maker's name,
They would ask their god for rain and our slight would be excused.

I had been leader seven years, so should we wish the air to clear,
The wicked priests would need to hear my voice call out their maker's
name.

I walked through blinding smoke to shore, fell to my knees beside my sword,

The priests assured me a reward would come, but all I sensed was shame.

I opened my mouth wide to say their maker's name but hesitated.

Thinking of my own true faith, I whispered out to Peace instead.

I heard not Peace, nor any voice, assisting me with any choices.

While the priests sang and rejoiced, tears for the gaoler Peace were shed.

Still, from smoke cloud I emerged, armed with not but sword and word,

Afraid of mostly what I'd heard, and what my heart had planned to say.

My voice cut windows through the cloud and to my will the mighty bowed

For they felt equally as proud of my intentions not to pray.

Into the war I called out "Why?" watched my cries flutter to the sky,

And when they couldn't fly that high, I watched them sink into our souls.

No deeper question could we find. No stronger hearts could wartime bind.

We all knew deep inside our minds the gaoler Peace had lost control.

Still, from fury I pulled strength, my sword held out at armor's length,

I bid my farewells to the saints and led my men into the clash.

We marched, and sped into a run, feet thumping with the sound of drums.

The blood and dust blocked out the sun while premonitions blocked our pasts.

The bravest hearts bled mighty blood, the priests called often for their gods,
And when the heavens answered not, they took up swords and joined the fray.
At that point fighting should have ceased, for they had clearly been defeated.
Bloodlust escaped the gaoler Peace and far too many died that day.

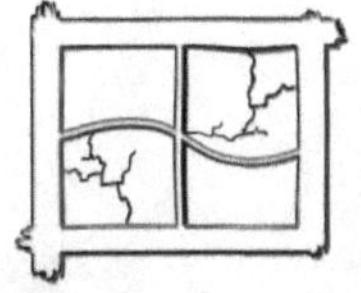

CIRCUMSTANCE

I am drifting
Towards the sun.
Much like the theory I once held
That the Earth
Is drifting from.
The shadowed moon is guiding me,
Much like the sea,
And thrusting me
Towards destiny.
No smarter smite than circumstance.
I find myself here
Not by chance,
But by own my will to
Survive.
I turn
And there before my eyes
The shuttle's explosive demise.
If I had stayed
I would have died.
My crew.

By these
Two words
My eyes shut closed.
And part
To let one teardrop roll.
Enough to make me lose control.
To have them back
I'd sell my soul.
Am I mad?
This soul I claim
Will soon belong to hellish flames.
Or have I died yet?
Did I forget?
I don't recall the pain...

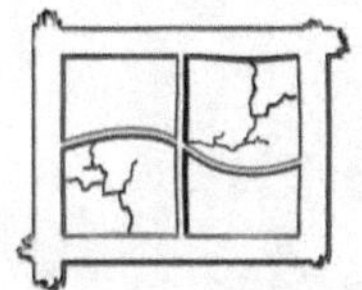

BIRDS AND SUCH

"So, what's the matter now?" They asked as I fell through the sky.
"I haven't got a parachute. I know I'm going to die."
Most people freefall constantly and never wonder why.
"You'll never find your happiness until you learn to fly."
I'm finding out that time is funny.
Birds and such fly by.

"You're going to hit the ground," they said, as I kept plummeting.
I'm well aware of gravity; it is a funny thing.
It may not even notice me. What would it want from me?
"I'm searching for lost happiness. In clouds I'm rummaging.
If you are finding yourself lonely,
Why not come with me?"

"Not too much longer now," they said, as Earth came into view.
"I'm looking forward to impact. it means I'm free of you."
And as my blood mixes with dirt, I'll know the myths are true.
No one can bounce when tumbling down from in a sky so blue.
My body will soon mix back in with
Dust from which I grew.

"Be careful where you land," they said, as ants turned into cars.
"My target is beneath me, so it can't be very far."
I have had little practice tossing bodies from the stars.
"Don't bother calling 911; I won't need C.P.R.
There isn't much else left to say
Aside from 'Au revoir'."

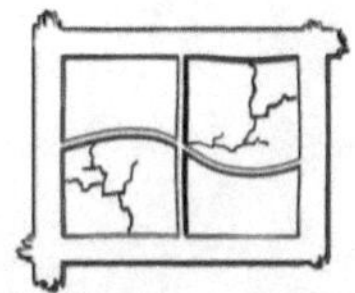

FIREWORKS

As the stars

Dimmed and elevated

Making room

For extravagant explosions

We ascended

To the rooftop

Vaguely similar

To the year before

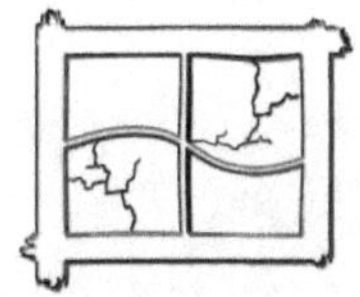

DORVAN

Sticky red blood.
It boils when I breathe.
They came here to stick me with swords they unsheathed
Outside of my den.

Miles from the cave,
On fallen, dried leaves,
I heard them approaching with helmets and greaves,
And torches as well.

Sticky red blood
And buzzing fly wings.
Deep sleep is a shade of the solace death brings.
I tire of men.

Always they come,
For glory, for kings,
Attacking me. Men are such horrible things.
A dragon can tell.

Sticky red blood.
Like rubies, it shines.
A spark from a torch and my breath intertwine
Erupting in flame.

Nothing remains
Save armor outlines
I search through the bone and the ashes to find
A treasure to keep.

Sticky red blood
Once covered these jewels.
Would-be hero knights are just covetous fools
Who know me by name.

More will be sent
By despots who rule
To take from the Dragon called Dorvan the Cruel.
Kings sow and I reap.

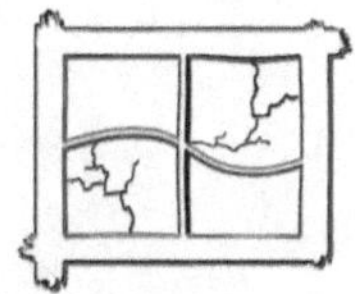

THE ORIGAMI PARADIGM

I found a little paper,
   And had a little time.
When I was done a brand new universe
Had left my mind.
I folded it into the
Origami Paradigm
So it resembled all the other worlds
I'd left behind.

And when they come unfolded
Every paper will reveal
The Origami stories that within
Have been concealed.
Each story, long and layered,
Waiting to become unpeeled
So they resemble all the other worlds
That feel so real.

ABOUT THE AUTHOR

R.E. Lockett is a fresh voice in contemporary narrative poetry. With a background in Literature and a passion for songwriting, Lockett draws inspiration from literary giants like Edgar Allan Poe, W.B. Yeats, Shel Silverstein, and Robert Frost.

He is the author and illustrator of three beloved children's books: *The Race to Flutter Flower Field*, *Monet and the Monster Magic*, and *Bear Bridge*.

Thin Windows marks his first collection of poetry. In this captivating work, Lockett transports readers to fantastical realms—from the rekindling of the sun to the haunting echoes of zombie Atlantis—where the lines between reality and imagination blur.